Scarlet and the White Wolf

Book 4: The King of Forever

KIRBY CROW

This is a work of fiction. Names, characters, places, and incidents are products of the author's imagination. Any resemblance to actual events or locales or persons, living or dead, is entirely coincidental.

Scarlet and the White Wolf, Book 4: The King of Forever

http://KirbyCrow.com
Bonecamp Books – 2016 Revised Edition

ISBN-13: 978-1542904940
ISBN-10: 1542904943
Cover Art by Kirby Crow

CONTENTS

1	Secrets and Silver	Pg	1
2	Ritual and Light	Pg	10
3	The Grove	Pg	22
4	Less Talking	Pg	38
5	Fire and Burning	Pg	96
6	Fading Dreams	Pg	151
7	Bread and Roses	Pg	171
8	Forever	Pg	204

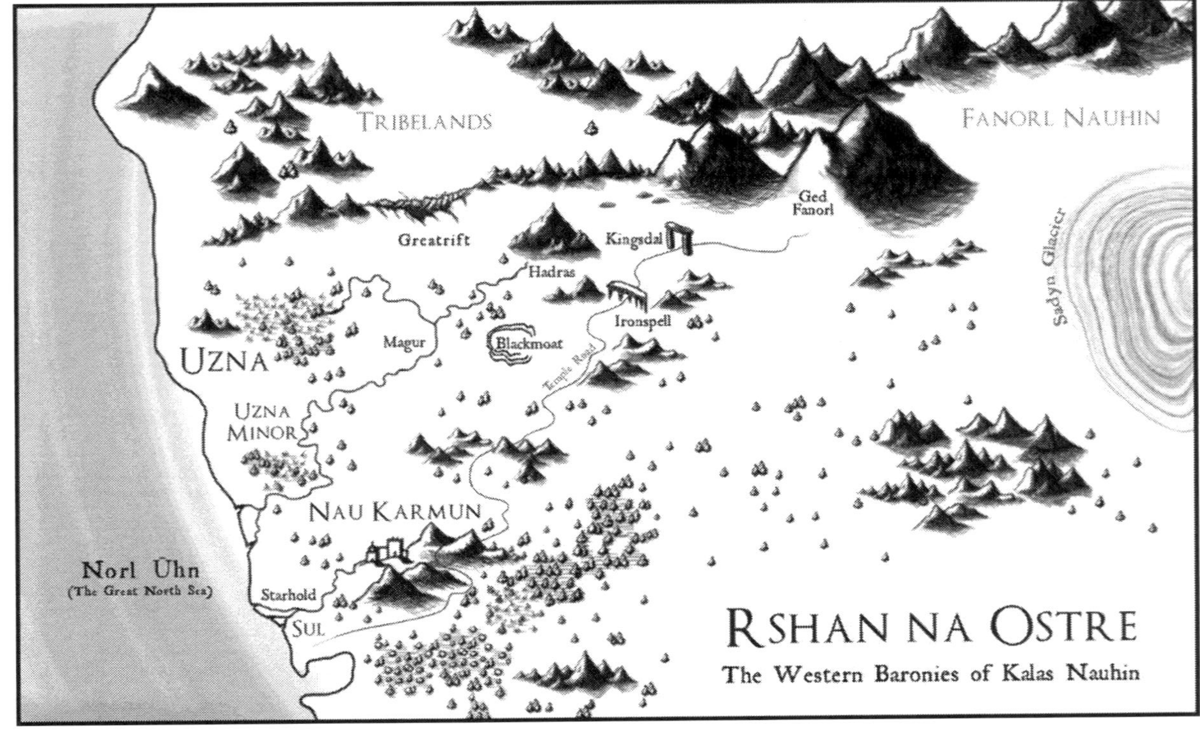
TRIBELANDS
FANORL NAUHIN
Ged Fanorl
Greatrift
Kingsdal
Hadras
Sadyn Glacier
Ironspell
Magur
Blackmoat
UZNA
Temple Road
UZNA MINOR
NAU KARMUN
Norl Ūhn
(The Great North Sea)
Starhold
SUL
RSHAN NA OSTRE
The Western Baronies of Kalas Nauhin

Prologue

The floor of the cave angled steeply down into the heart of the frozen mountain. Milky blue stalactites, brittle as flint, clung perilously to the ceiling as the king entered, wind howling at his back.

The barrier was broken, its hinges snapped and the great iron gates flung wide. He hesitated, torn with doubt. There was so much to risk, but so much more to gain. The risk troubled him less than he feared it would. His lands and castles were gone, passed on to lesser heirs without the wit to manage them, his sons long dead, himself exiled without comfort or aid. Now the Kinslayer had returned to claim what he did not deserve.

Deva. Om-Ret. Senkhara.

No, he had little luxury now to fret over *risk.*

Ramung entered the Kingsdal and looked upon the frozen faces of the great kings and queens entombed inside the ice; their noble features, their white hair and staring blue eyes. They looked nearly alive, paused in the midst of speaking. He wondered if they would have wished him well on his quest, or if they would have cursed him.

"Pail'aa sest Nauhin," he said. *For the Shining Ones.* The invocation was as old as the cavern itself, perhaps. Who knew how many thousands of years ago the Shining Ones had arrived on this world with hope in their hearts, only to find a land locked in ice and all life ravenous to devour them. Their

magic had sustained them for many seasons, but so had the vessel.

The vessel. He must not forget her. When the magic of the Shining Ones waned, the benevolent vessel shattered her consciousness into three fragments. She sent two of these shards to explore the world, to find the keys to survival and return with the knowledge. The Shining Ones began their long wait with only their little companions, the Anlyribeth, to bolster their dying powers. After many years, even that connection began to wither, and still the fragments did not return.

Whatever Deva's other minds found in the vast reaches of the world, it was too potent to allow them to return to the mountain. The shards became gods in their new lands, as all great magic-wielders do.

Deva. Om-Ret. Senkhara.

The Anlyribeth, so secretive and clever, used their magic to adapt seamlessly to the world. Even with her consciousness broken and dispersed, Deva continued to aid them and ensure their survival after their masters turned cruel. When the Anlyribeth threw off their chains and fled, she went with them, leaving the Shining Ones powerless and undefended, at the mercy of the elements.

Deva was not only a traitor, she was heartless.

Abandoned, the Shining Ones required a new source of life. They could either merge with the world or be destroyed by it. They chose the merging, and the Ancients were the result. From the Ancients sprang the Rshani, leaving only the Anlyribeth unchanged by the passage of time, or nearly so.

Ramung traced his hand over a pane of blue ice, so clear it appeared like a wall of topaz. Columns of cone-shaped stalagmites jutted up from the floor like teeth, a maw to swallow up his past. He smelled strange scents in the cave: a whiff of burning tar, the sour tang of rusted metal, and one odor so foreign that he had no name for it. Other impressions came to him: salt and heated glass, the musty stink of old garments. Tiny lights winked in the darkness, a deep thrum like a heartbeat vibrated against the walls, and he heard faint, rhythmic sounds, as if small birds were chirping in unison. There was a pattern to it…

Deep in the gloom of the mountain, Ramung saw a pair of great yellow eyes glowing in the darkness, and he gave himself to them.

Secrets and Silver

The pile of bloody bear skins was growing larger.

"There are more today than yesterday," Liall remarked.

Alexyin's thick braid was a banner of white on the breast of his brilliant sapphire virca. He kept pace with the king by staying a scant step behind on his left.

"They seek to honor your name day, my lord, and to show their hope for the future." He pinched his hooked nose, nostrils drawn in fastidiously against the tangy smell of both fresh and rotting hides.

"Hope and blood seldom go well together. I need soldiers, not pelts." The king turned his head, and although he was a tall man, he had to look up a little to meet Alexyin's eyes.

Nazheradei, known as Liall the Wolf in Kalaslyn and as Kinslayer among his own people, was lean and broad-shouldered, with jutting cheekbones and amber skin. His pale blue eyes were fringed with thick silver lashes, his white hair bound at the nape of his neck. He cut a royal figure, clad in a rich virca sparkling with precious jewels, but he wore it uncomfortably.

They were the only two in the hall. The palace corridors were empty, all the visiting jackals tucked away in their lavish rooms, waiting.

Waiting is what scavengers do best, Liall thought bitterly. *After the ceremony, a war council, and after that…*

He shook his head. Leave tomorrow for tomorrow. He hadn't even gotten through the damned morning yet.

"If you'd let them have a day of celebration, there might be no pelts," Alexyin hinted. Since Cestimir's murder, Alexyin had served as Chamberlain, while Nenos was House Marus, the keeper of the king's household. Bhakamir, the handsome and capable courtier who had served Liall's mother, had returned to the Setna.

"Now is not the time for frivolous celebrations. The day of my birth is just another day. They may celebrate Scarlet's name day, if they wish."

Alexyin's dour mouth turned down even further. His face was graven with deep lines, not all from age. "And when is that?"

"You know, I'm not entirely sure. I believe he was born in winter, though Hilurin count years by summers they've seen, and not by exact dates."

"It must be because they can't read."

"They can count, I assure you. Scarlet can."

"Like all merchants. But it's a rare talent for a peasant, I'll grant."

Liall clenched his teeth at the dismissive tone. "I remind you, my old friend, that ser Keriss is a noble of my court, with a rank higher than any baron you'd give deference to without hesitation. You will esteem his position, at the least, and not force me to defend him to you again." He glanced sideways at Alexyin and his voice grew softer. "Even Jochi has said he has never met a finer young man than Scarlet. It grieves me that you can't find it in you to care for him just a little. He is worthy of your friendship."

Alexyin turned his face away. "Yes, my lord."

He still blames Scarlet for Cestimir's death, Liall thought. He would have to deal with that at some point.

But not today.

A wide corridor led away from the royal tier, its stone walls covered in the blue banners of Camira-Druz. Their steps turned toward it, pacing over star-patterned tiles gleaming with polish. Scarlet would have called the halls chilly, even with the daylight fires roaring in every hearth, but Liall found them quite warm. Winter ended today. There would be a Greentide feast, and soon, the gods willing, a good harvest.

"With so many bears taken, the roads will be safer this spring, at least," Alexyin pointed out.

"So some good will come of courtly gestures, other than a lady's smile." Liall wrinkled his nose. "Don't forget to have someone collect those skins. They're beginning to smell."

"And ser Keriss is not overly fond of looking at them."

"He hates the sight and I don't blame him. I've never been bowled over by a snow bear, but I can sympathize with how it must have felt. Get rid of them. Have them cured. Burn them with ceremony. I care not."

"I will attend to the matter, sire."

Liall slowed his steps as they neared the great armored doors to the outer courtyard. "I'm not looking forward to the war council."

"Then don't hold one."

"Is that your advice? I didn't elevate you to chamberlain only to hear *yes* from your lips. You've been damnably silent on the subject."

Alexyin shrugged eloquently. "You ceased to crave my approval when you were still a boy, my lord. At any rate, I am a chamberlain, not a soldier, and the emissaries of the barons are already here."

"Which is neither an answer nor an opinion. Don't be cagey with me. If I'd wanted coy responses, I'd have sent for Jochi."

"And where is my kinsman today?"

Another change of subject. "With Tesk. I've set them to a task." Because it was Alexyin, Liall did not explain that the task was to begin forming a company of men to wear Scarlet's badge and be his formal guard. Like Alexyin, Jochi was also a Setna, and because Setna were excellent spies, Alexyin would know soon enough what the task was.

Setna, the old order of the wise, the brotherhood dedicated to preserving the knowledge of the Ancients and protecting the royal line through counsel. Some were also assassins, agents, and informers, but their training was rigorous. After they were released from apprenticeship at the Blackmoat and allowed to serve the crown, their loyalty was unquestionable. A Setna *served*, as Alexyin had served Prince Cestimir and Jochi had served the queen. Cestimir was dead, murdered by Vladei, which had opened the way for Liall to be crowned king. It was a thing he had neither sought nor desired, but now that it had come to him, he had no intention of giving it up.

"Tesk's silver tongue is legendary. He could winkle out a monk's secrets."

"Silver," Liall murmured. "If only the Ava Thule could be bought with silver. Alas, you can't eat metal. Coin means nothing in the far north. I'll wager you couldn't trade ten silver bars for a haunch of rabbit in Whitehell."

Alexyin cleared his throat. "Speaking of rabbits, my lord… I'm running out of game to set loose on the palace grounds."

"Send for more. Discreetly. If ser Keriss discovers his hunts are salted, he will not be amused."

"I had a thought," Alexyin ventured. "In the hunting lands you granted him, there is a small grove where I *could* set loose some larger game."

"Not reindeer, I trust."

"Deer? No. Too large to be brought down with a bow his size. I thought perhaps an ice fox or a snowy grouse."

Slightly bigger game, and harder to hunt. There were trees and bracken within the grove for the game to hide, and enough foliage and ruins to interest Scarlet's exploring nature. Liall nodded in agreement. "Nothing dangerous. Accidents can happen on any hunt. Jochi can go, too. Scarlet will want to know the names of the trees and such."

"The Hilurin is a born forester," Alexyin said in uncommon praise. "He never forgets a tree or a flower, and yet the Sinha language escapes him."

As usual, the praise had turned to slight. "It's a different kind of learning," Liall said, nettled.

"Our language is too complex. He will never be able to do more than muddle along in it."

"He needs more time. It is no matter, either way. Enough Rshani speak Bizye in the Nauhinir, and I speak it like a mother tongue." He looked at Alexyin to watch his reaction. "I even dream in it sometimes."

Alexyin blew through pursed lips in displeasure. "Best not to let *that* get around."

"I intend to keep it to myself, henceforth." They rounded a sharp corner and saw far down the hall a pair of barred doors where a brace of guards stood watchfully with immense, steel-tipped spears in their hands. The spear-tips crossed over the doors, barring exit or entry.

Liall took a deep breath. "This should have been Cestimir's duty," he said quietly.

"Should, but is not. And it is not duty, but honor." They were at the doors. The guards parted their spears.

Alexyin reached for Liall's collar to adjust his formal virca and brushed a bit of lint from his shoulder. Liall smiled at the familiarity.

Satisfied with the king's appearance, Alexyin nodded. "Bring back the sun."

Liall had never deluded himself that he could read Alexyin perfectly, or that he knew all there was to know about him, but the man's stubborn rejection of Scarlet was bewildering. Vladei had been a formidable enemy, far beyond Scarlet's capabilities to deal with. Partnered with an Ancient as powerful as Melev, neither Scarlet nor Cestimir had stood a chance. Why couldn't Alexyin see that?

"Alexyin," Liall said gently. "My friend. It was a sleigh ride. Two boys being boys. Nothing more."

Alexyin folded his hands. "Of course, my lord."

Liall sighed and let it go. The time to heal the rift between his old teacher and his beloved was not when he had a host of riders waiting. He gestured and the doors parted.

Twenty guards seated on matched silver mounts waited in a blue, freezing dawn. The land had been in twilight for months, but today the giant stars of the Longwalker constellation shone bright and brilliant in the sky, lighting their way. Liall spied Scarlet astride a dappled gray pony in the center of the column, draped in furs and muffled to the nose.

Scarlet saw him, pulled the furs down from his face and grinned. The knot in Liall's chest eased.

"Remember what we've spoken of," he said quietly to Alexyin, watching Scarlet. "We will not have that conversation again."

Alexyin glanced at Scarlet. His gaze turned distant and he bent his head. "As my king commands."

Liall stared at him. It was Alexyin's shape and form, but he did not know the voice. It was so formal, so bitter.

Liall turned his back and went to Scarlet and the waiting guards, but his spine tingled and his blood was chilled. What had he heard in Alexyin's voice?

When the wind sent skirls of snow over his boots and

the groom came forward to offer him the reins, Liall knew. It was *cold.* Alexyin was cold through to the marrow. When had that happened?

When dear cousin Vladei cut off Cestimir's head.

Alexyin had never married. He had no children. To Liall's knowledge, he had truly loved only one person, and that was the murdered prince.

If it were I who had lost his hope and his life's work, would I turn as wintry inside as Alexyin? What if I lost Scarlet?

Nadei's face in the last moment he had seen him alive bloomed in Liall's mind. His brother had looked so surprised to see blood pooling around his feet, his lips turning ashen, and all he could say was, *"Oh."* As if he had never expected the day to go so wrong.

Thank Deva there were no more royal siblings to slaughter each other for the crown, only that sneaking Eleferi, who was scarcely a threat. Eleferi might be fated to meet the same end as Vladei, but it would not be by his hand. Liall had borne the title of Kinslayer for sixty years. Never again.

For a terrible moment, the deathly cold threatened to slip inside him, to claim a place and leech strength from him to grow.

In the distance, from the craggy cliffs surrounding the palace, he heard a wolf pack calling. The howls filled him with loneliness. He busied himself with the harness and mounting the saddle, and then Scarlet was beside him. The darkness passed.

Scarlet's black eyes shone and his smooth cheeks blushed apple-red with cold.

Liall smiled. "Good morning, beautiful."

I will not lose him, he vowed silently. *I will not.*

Ritual and Light

The blue twilight that had endured all through the winter dimly illuminated the land spread out below the mesa in a thousand shades of indigo. The great valley was a smooth floor of ice ringed by white hills and jagged black cliffs. Winding through the valley like a silver snake was an endless, shining road, smooth as a calm river.

From horseback, Liall pointed. "The Temple Road," he said. "Do you not recognize it? It begins at the sea and wends up here through the passes of the Nauhinir, then goes all the way to the sacred mountain of Ged Fanorl."

Scarlet patted the wild mane of his horse and peered into the distance. He didn't like to think about that road. He wondered if they had ever recovered Cestimir's broken sleigh from it.

Unlike Liall, who rode a sleek stallion, Scarlet's stout, shaggy mount was considered a pony in Rshan. In Byzantur, it could have carried a large man. He made his voice careless. "How far is that?"

"Leagues and leagues."

Scarlet arched his brows. "You don't know?"

Liall held the reins loosely in one hand and smiled. "I confess, I do not. It's been many years since I've had reason to count them. I've spent more of my life in Byzantur than I have in Rshan."

In Byzantur, Liall had claimed that Norl Udur was his homeland. Only when they were on the ship did he reveal that Norl Udur was actually Rshan na Ostre, a land Scarlet's people believed to be a myth, the home of gods and giants.

The high, flat mesa could have afforded them a stunning view, if they were not surrounded by a black circle of standing stones three times the height of a man. A cadre of spear-toting royal guards in full regalia waited patiently outside the stones for them, within earshot but keeping a respectful distance.

"I've never gotten dressed up to look at the sky before," Scarlet said. A thick silver brooch at his throat held the fur cloak pinned together, and beneath that, he wore a fine blue virca embroidered with Liall's house emblem of stars. A cold wind blew from the north and the stars seemed to pale in the sky.

"This damn thing itches," Liall complained, shrugging his broad shoulders inside his own heavy formal virca. The leather saddle beneath him creaked with his weight and the horse whickered.

Scarlet looked at the king, admiring the cut of his profile, his sharp cheekbones and snowy hair, and the deep color of his skin, like polished oak. Though most Rshani shared similar traits, Scarlet never tired of looking at this particular one. "At least you're well-protected. There's enough silver and gems on that to pass for armor."

"I look like a peacock in mating season," Liall groused.

"No one can see us except the rocks and the horses."

"There are the guards. And the entire Nauhinir when we

ride back."

"You complain much."

Liall went on as if he hadn't heard. "I think this virca weighs more than you do."

Scarlet winked. "When this is over, I'll see what I can do about getting you out of it."

Liall laughed, then cleared his throat and straightened his back. "It won't be long now."

"What should I do?"

"Pretend to concentrate on the east. Draw your brows together in a frown. Be ever-so-serious." Liall winked back.

Scarlet studied the valley below. His fingers went to his brooch and he traced the outlines of it. It was a snow bear, exquisitely molded. "I never imagined that snow and ice could hold so many colors."

Liall glanced at him. "Your sight is truly amazing. I can only see shades of blue and gray, but I'm not a Hilurin."

"I forgive you."

The king smirked.

Scarlet had only seen the Temple Road as far as the ruins where Cestimir had died, and never from such a high vantage point. He narrowed his eyes and peered into the distant hills. "I don't see anything that looks like a sacred mountain."

"You cannot. You can't even see the Blackmoat from here. We'd have to travel far past that ridge," Liall pointed to a line of dark cliffs, so distant that Scarlet could have blotted them out with his thumb, "and take the Temple Road through the valley on the other side to get to the home of the Setna."

"I've never seen a road like that. Doesn't look natural." The road was raised yet appeared to be smooth and level, every curve precise and perfect. Scarlet looked to Liall for answers.

Liall shrugged. "The Ancients made the Temple Road, or so the legend goes. Other stories say that the road was here long before them, and the Shining Ones who raised the standing stones still wait inside the ice, longing for the sun to return."

"Are there more of these stones?" Scarlet looked down at the snow beneath his horse's hooves. *Inside* the ice?

"This is the largest, but there are many such circles and markers in the far north, and monoliths, too. We think there are many we haven't found, and many that lie in the deep places, in ice caves and massive rifts in the earth." Liall nodded his head to the north, where the humped blue and white shapes became strange and hard for the eye to follow. "If we were to venture out there, we might find such things, but few who leave the Temple Road survive. The land is treacherous. Nenos used to tell me it is angry, and that it grows hungry and yearns to devour travelers. But when we travel, the road keeps us safe. Or so the stories say."

"Did the Ancients build it for themselves?" Scarlet was disturbed by the talk of hungry earth. He looked left and right, but could see nothing moving.

Liall shook his head. "For us, for the Rshani. The road was to lead their descendants out from Fanorl to the sea. There was a time when we, too, lived deep in the center of the continent, but the land was too cruel. The Ancients had to forge a way south for us when we became too many to sustain ourselves. Melev once said that the Ancients were most pleased that their children were so fond of breeding, but they hated crowding, so they built a road to the sun."

Scarlet frowned at the mention of Melev. If not for Melev, perhaps Cestimir would still be alive. He was not sure who he blamed more for the murder, Melev or Vladei. He was certain of one thing: Vladei had held the sword, but Melev had made it all possible.

"If they'd done that, you'd have ended up in Byzantur," Scarlet said. "I wouldn't exactly call Kalas Nauhin *sunny.*"

"Near enough. Ancients hate the water, but we don't."

"You do."

Liall chuckled. "I thought we'd cleared that up? I don't hate the water; I just hate being at the mercy of another's skill rather than my own. I'm no mariner. Anyway, I'm not your ordinary Rshani." He gave Scarlet a questioning look. "These are tales any child should know. I thought Jochi was teaching you history?"

Scarlet made a rude noise. "He does, but your lot never runs out of history. Muckety Muck married Muck and they had many mucklings, and then there was war." He made talking motions with one hand. "Yap yap yap. After a while, all the names run together and sound like babbling water. I can't tell one Lyran Something who lived a thousand years ago from one who lived a hundred years ago."

"Lyran is an old family name. I have many ancestors named Lyran. I always told my mother that if I had a son one day…" The words trailed off. "Never mind. It's not a good day to talk of past or future. Let's do as the snow bears do and live in the moment. Today, I have no past."

If he has a son. Scarlet's mood plummeted. *The only way he's going to get a son is if he marries Ressilka.*

In the months since Liall had taken the throne, while the deep winter passed, there had been whispers of putting the Lady Ressilka forward as the future queen of Rshan. There had been no formal betrothal while Cestimir was alive, but everyone knew that if Cestimir had lived, Ressilka would have been his queen. So far, Scarlet had been able to ignore the gossip. Liall's careful avoidance of the subject informed him that he wasn't the only one getting an earful.

"No," Scarlet said adamantly. "That's no way to start thinking. I'm not a bear and neither are you." Liall shot him a cryptic look but said nothing, and Scarlet wondered what it meant.

Scarlet tugged the fur collar of the cloak over his mouth as the wind began to draw tears from his eyes. "Tell me about one of these famous Lyran people," he said, his voice muffled. "Start with the best one."

Liall sidled his horse closer to Scarlet's. "It's a male name. Lyran was one of the last of the Druz. My family is actually two families who came together after a long war, the Camira and the Druz, hence my name. He was a great peacemaker, a wise king who brought a warring people together and saved them from destruction. They say Lyran had the look of the old Druz, as tall as an Ancient, with hair so white it held shades of blue and violet, and eyes bright as a candle flame."

"Jochi has yellow eyes."

"I would say more gold than yellow, but yes, he does. His bloodline is old." Liall tugged at his long white bangs. His hair had grown past his shoulders in their months in Rshan. "Many of our women have some gold in their hair, but generally there is little variation in our coloring. Silver and blue: those are the colors of Rshan."

"In banners and people both," Scarlet quipped. "Except Ressilka. She has hair almost like a Morturii, but she's taller than any Morturii man."

Liall's mouth turned down, and he nodded. "You're not the first one to make note of that. Ressanda's ancestor was Maksha, a mariner. Maksha was in love with a beautiful Morturii dancer, and when they had a child, he obtained the crown's permission to bring both mother and child home with him. Maksha named his daughter Romaksha, after him, and she became a famous dancer in Rshan. Although she was a half-blooded commoner, she had no shortage of noble suitors vying for her hand. They said her hair fell to her ankles and was like a living flame."

"But how—" Scarlet frowned. "I'm sorry, I don't want to be rude, but I wondered. I know how your people feel about *lenilyn.*"

"So how did Romaksha find a husband, and a noble one at that?" Liall touched Scarlet's cheek softly. "I wish you would not use that word. *Lenilyn.* You know what it means."

He did, but he refused to hide from a *word.* "If it bothers you, I won't say it again."

"Rshani men have a weakness for beauty, as you know,"

Liall said, overlooking the barb. "It was scandalous, of course, but Romaksha married into a noble family of Tebet, and her son was Baron Ressanda's father. Ressanda, however, did not come to rule Tebet by right of blood. He married my cousin Winotheri, and *her* father was the rightful lord of Tebet."

"So why didn't she rule instead of him? Your mother ruled and she was a wondrous fine queen."

"Yes, but she was a *queen*, love. There are rules and there are rules, if you understand me."

Scarlet did not.

"What I mean is, there are rules for the people and there are rules for the Camira-Druz. We are…" Liall seemed to be searching for the right word. "I don't know if there's a way to explain it. You don't have a term for it in Bizye."

Scarlet's horse pricked his ears forward and shuffled his hooves restlessly, and Scarlet patted his mane to gentle him. "There's a first; you not having twenty words when one would do."

Liall smiled. "It's difficult to put the concept together succinctly, but in a sense, the Camira-Druz are to the Rshani what the Flower Prince is to Byzantur."

Scarlet looked at him quickly. "They believe the gods speak to you?"

"Hardly. Rather, they think we can intercede with something they revere, and in some ways, we can. An Ancient must come when a Camira-Druz calls."

Scarlet gave Liall a sour look. "I don't much care for your Ancients."

"Neither would I, if I'd gone through what you did. I don't say I forgive them, but just like men, not all Ancients are cut from the same cloth. I don't pretend to understand them, either, like I would never understand a Shining One."

Scarlet was curious all over again. He was always curious about the Shining Ones, who were honored among the Rshani but were demigods to the Hilurin, as well as demons. "Did the Shining Ones really come from this place?" He looked around him at the barren but strangely alive landscape. The vast expanse of ice and snow never seemed to stop changing. Perhaps it really was alive and restless, like the stories Liall mentioned. The wind had died down and he could hear the deep, healthy breathing of the horses and the faint clinks of armor and the weapons of the guards.

"All the stories tell us is that they emerged from Ged Fanorl, which is a mountain to the north," Liall said. "Though we have never seen them, we sense them. The Ancients are our link to them, to our origins. There could have been no Rshani as a people without the Ancients."

There were large gaps in Scarlet's knowledge about Liall's people, but he was beginning to realize there was much *they* did not know, either. It seemed there were mysteries that not even the Setna were able or willing to reveal, and all Rshani hated to admit ignorance. He'd never met a people more proud of themselves.

A shadow drifted through the valley, moving rapidly.

"*Liall!*" Scarlet called in alarm. His muscles tensed and he sawed on the horse's reins. The horse shied and balked in fear.

Liall quickly seized the reins and stopped the horse from

bolting. "It's all right," he murmured. "It's fine."

"I saw something." Scarlet jerked the fur collar from his face and pointed. "There on the ice. It was…" He shook his head and his breath quickened to a fog before his eyes. "It had *arms,* I think. Or something. I don't know what it was. It moved so fast."

"We're safe," Liall said. He touched Scarlet's shoulder. "Pay it no mind. It is not aware of us. We matter nothing to it."

"It?" Scarlet felt his hands shaking. "Is it a monster?" He recalled their voyage across the oceans and the huge, fanged fish that Liall and the mariners had hunted before they reached the ice. He had thought those were monsters, too, but Liall had laughed and said they were only fish.

Liall looked over Scarlet's head into the distance, narrowing his eyes. "No," he said, though he did not sound all that sure. "But it is not something we should disturb. It will not harm us."

"What is it?"

"Call it a wind rider. That's the closest I can get to the term in Bizye."

"It flies?"

"Not really. Glides, more like. Stop looking over your shoulder. It won't come all the way up here. I told you: we do not matter to it. It can't eat us and we're not interesting enough to get its attention."

"A wind rider," Scarlet murmured. He felt colder. "What does it eat?"

"Ice, if the tales are true. Look!" Liall pointed to the east, a note of excitement in his voice. "There it is. I told you, redbird."

Scarlet's breath caught in his throat. After so long, it had seemed he would never look upon such a sight again. A razor-edge of orange, vivid as fire against the monochrome landscape, hovered on the rim of the horizon. It shimmered and flared like a live thing, and as he watched, the band of fire grew larger and a shaft of light burst through the surrounding trees, arrowing down between the circle of black stones.

"Gentle Deva," Scarlet breathed. He could see the sun.

Liall chuckled. "So your Byzan legends are only partially true. This *is* the land of night, but it's also the land of the sun. Get used to looking at that, t'aishka. You'll be seeing it in Kalas Nauhin until fall." He called out in Sinha to their guards, his voice loud and merry, and the guards answered with happy shouts and a rhyming cheer in Sinha that Scarlet caught two words of: *shining* and *green*.

"What did you tell them?"

"Just that the sun had returned. It's officially spring, or Greentide as we call it." Liall sighed in satisfaction and turned his horse's head toward the waiting guards and the road back to the Nauhinir. "Now the ice will melt in the straights and the eastern barons will be free to come to the palace and make their pledges to the crown."

"Will they come?" Scarlet asked.

"Oh yes," Liall said, very confident.

"When?"

"Soon." He winked. "After all, if the king can call the

sun, he ought to be able to manage a pack of mortal barons."

The Grove

Scarlet raised his arm and pointed to a spot in the sky, low on the horizon. "What's that?" he asked Jochi lazily. A yellow blur hovered just above the trees, barely visible through heavy snow clouds.

"That is the sun, ser," Jochi answered, polite as ever. He sent a hard look to the armored Nauhinir guards who had accompanied the hunting party to the gate of the grove, as if daring them to laugh.

They were on the hunting lands that Liall had gifted to Scarlet. For six months, the sky had been either a dome of indigo dotted with stars or a heavy cover of solid clouds which could barely be seen against the dark. Occasionally, the *ostre sul,* the lights in the darkness, had illuminated the sky with brilliant bands of blue and green, and sometimes orange, purple, yellow, or even red. Jochi claimed these lights could be predicted, but whatever method the Setna used was unknown to Scarlet. He only knew they were wondrous, and he was a little sad when he was told that they would be very difficult to see until Greentide—the Rshani spring and summer—was over.

Scarlet only questioned Jochi to be difficult. For days, he had been expecting the season to turn into the bright, blazing summers he had known in Byzantur, and he was bitterly disappointed that the sun stubbornly refused to spill more than this milky half-light upon the land. For sure, this summer sun never set, but how could anything grow under it?

"Is it the same sun we have back home?" he wondered. It seemed impossible that the little blob of light that skated around the horizon but never seemed to rise in the sky was the great bronze sun that had warmed his back as a child.

"The very same." Jochi slipped off his mount and held the reins of Scarlet's pony for him while he dismounted. "It is as much daylight as we can expect this month, ser. It may snow again later."

It had snowed yesterday. Or last night. Scarlet was finding it every bit as hard to keep track of hours when the sun never set as he did when it never rose. He patted his gray pony on the nose. "The tracks will be fresh. Easier to hunt."

"Yes, ser."

"I don't like easy."

Scarlet unslung Whisper from his back and looked down. There were rabbit tracks leading off into the grove.

The hunting lands Liall had given him were a few hundred acres of rambling, forested hills. Scarlet's favorite part of it was the grove, a wide meadow dotted with apple trees and bordered by low stone walls that ran for many acres and circled it all around except for one gate.

Hunting the grove was like spearing fish in a barrel. Scarlet preferred simply to walk there and admire the trees, but he was restless and eager for any sport, no matter how tame.

He strung one end of his bow and slipped it between his

knees while standing, then he bent one limb far back to loop the string to the other bow nock.

Jochi watched him. "There is nothing *easy* about pinning a running rabbit with an arrow, ser."

The Nauhinir guards in their hunting party exchanged looks. Tesk, the handsome artist and courtier, cleared his throat.

Scarlet looked at the royal painter. "Have I said something wrong?"

Tesk wore a brilliant green virca embroidered with bright birds giving chase to butterflies. The green leather bracer on his left arm bore a hawk emblem. Liall had granted Tesk an additional appointment as royal Falconer; an undemanding job that would not interfere with his art, but allowed him to accompany Scarlet on the hunt without gossip from the court. Privately, Scarlet thought Jochi would have made a better falconer, but Liall said that Jochi had asked to remain a simple courtier and tutor, so his position remained the same: companion to the king's household.

And making Tesk the falconer is as good as saying he's my new wet nurse, Scarlet thought. *I don't mind. He's pleasant company, and like Jochi, he never grows weary of questions.*

"There are few in the Nauhinir graced with your skill, ser Keriss," Tesk said. His page sat astride a gelding and held a large, hooded gyrfalcon on his gauntlet, though they were not hunting with birds today. "The bow is a weapon of war, yes, but one requiring a delicate touch. You'll not find a great deal of delicacy in the men of the Nauhinir. Theor, for instance, whom I often mistake for a rampaging bear. Warriors employ either the crossbow or something… bigger." Tesk smiled charmingly. He was always charming.

"You mean a bow big enough to punch through a giant. I'd like to see one of those." Scarlet liked Tesk. Most of what he said was gossip or nonsense, but he never took on airs or tried to make anyone feel lesser.

Scarlet selected an arrow from the quiver strapped to his back. He didn't need to look. He could tell from touch which were the slender bodkin arrows for small game and which were the notched broadheads for larger targets. The largest game he had encountered in the grove was a snow fox with eyes of startling blue, so beautiful that he'd let it go, but Liall had mentioned that deer had been seen in the grove over the winter.

"I can't stretch one of your crossbows," he said. "I'd be fighting it all day and in the end, the bow would win. I'd be snarled like a ball of yarn."

Tesk unslung his weapon—an ash longbow twice the length of Scarlet's recurve—and dismounted. "I can't hit a fleeing rabbit, so we are even, ser." He slipped an arrow from his quiver and nodded to the field. "Shall we?"

Scarlet glanced to Jochi. There were many complicated rules about who could keep company with a king's consort, but he hadn't learned them all. Liall had handily side-stepped those rules by making Tesk his falconer. While Scarlet enjoyed the artist's easy mood and frequent smiles, he was curious to see if Tesk could stalk game silently. He doubted it.

Jochi handed the reins to a guard. "I'll come with you, ser."

"No, stay here and mind my horse," Scarlet answered.

"He likes you."

Jochi looked at Tesk and then back to Scarlet. "Ser, I should come. And the guards, as well. It is my duty—"

"Aren't you a little young to be such an old hen?" Scarlet winked at Jochi. "We won't wander very far, and besides, you'd scare the game. I don't think you've tracked anything smaller than a snow bear in your life."

"That has nothing to do with it."

"'Course it does. A bear doesn't run when it hears the hunter. This kind of hunt calls for stealth. Stay here."

Jochi's frown was formidable on such a noble face. "As you command, ser." He shot a warning look at Tesk, who returned his regard unruffled. "Please be careful."

"I will, never fear," Scarlet promised airily, knowing Jochi would fret himself into a lather whether he was careful or not. It was a miracle they didn't wrap him in wool and stuff him in a closet, like his mum tried to do with a doll once. A rich merchant with a broken wagon wheel had made a present of the doll to Annaya. His little sister adored it, lavishing kisses on the porcelain mouth, the expensive satin gown and garnet buttons. While Scaja had repaired the wheel, Linhona had carefully tucked the doll away for safekeeping until Annaya was older and less careless. Annaya found it, of course.

All in ashes, now. He frowned and shook his head, willing the darkness away.

"Are you well, ser?" Tesk asked.

Scarlet turned a sunny smile on the painter. "Never better."

He turned for the grove, but his pony whickered anxiously and pulled against the reins. Scarlet chuckled and scratched the pony's soft, gray ears.

"Enough of you, silly beast. You're getting plump and spoiled. Be good for Jochi and there's an apple in it for you." He glanced at Jochi. "I'll have to give him a name soon. What do you fancy I should call him?"

"Apples," Jochi said, deadpan.

Thick, leafless limbs of fruit trees, fringed with snow, made a lacy canopy over their heads. Scarlet cat-footed through a stone arch in the grove, the third of many such arches and pylons built over the centuries. He'd been comforted when Liall revealed that the markers denoted the location of graves.

"Not royal graves," Liall had said. "When royalty dies, they are taken to the Kingsdal, to be entombed and preserved in ice forever. The snows never melt in the far north."

Scarlet's village had contained an *afarit,* where the earthly remains of Hilurin were buried to nourish the fruit trees that grew there. Others preferred to be settled deep in their own grain fields. There had been a few tombstones in the afarit for those of non-Hilurin blood, and the wealthy could afford to consign their remains to the priests of Deva, who took them to charnel grounds high in the mountains for sky burials.

Scarlet yearned to ask Liall if he could build a small *templon* in the grove to honor his parents, but he knew that asking for a Hilurin shrine on Rshani land was an unwise request, one that Liall would want to grant anyway and they would both regret.

Tesk followed Scarlet a few paces back, being much more silent than Scarlet thought anyone with feet that big could manage. The ground crunched softly under their boots as they tracked the paw prints of a large hare. They went deeper into the grove, almost out of sight of their party. Scarlet could hear the breath of the horses still, and Jochi's low whispers as he spoke to the guards. If he could hear them, the game could.

He motioned to Tesk to follow him as he rounded a stand of apple trees. They roamed deeper into the silent woods for another quarter of an hour, their progress slow and quiet, until they were nearing the eastern wall of the grove.

Scarlet stopped under an apple tree. Most of its silver limbs were still bare, but on a low branch, several sprigs of bright green sprouted from the bark.

It had been so long since he saw budding green. Suddenly, he had an impulse to help it along. "Tesk," he whispered. He touched a finger to the branch and warmth flowed from his skin.

Tesk watched him curiously.

Scarlet leaned close to the tree and breathed a withy chant onto the tiny green leaves. They stirred, twisted, and bright pink buds popped into existence. They unfurled swiftly into white blossoms with blushing petals.

Tesk's eyes went round and he exhaled in awe.

"Amazing."

Scarlet smiled in real pleasure. He hadn't had much chance to use his Gift since he landed in Rshan, and almost none at all since Liall was made king. Smiling, he gave the withy another little push. *"On danaee Deva shani,"* he whispered.

It was too much.

The blossoms withered, dropped, and small, red fruits appeared, no bigger than his smallest fingernail. They weren't small for long. He stopped the withy in mid-chant and tried to pull back his Gift, but it wouldn't come.

He stepped away, hoping the distance would break the connection, but the apples kept growing. The slender branch bowed and snapped with a crack.

Scarlet stared in dismay at the ruined branch and the apples at his feet.

"Ser?" Worry was in Tesk's voice.

"That's not how that's supposed to happen," Scarlet murmured. He looked at the palm of his hand. "I've never been able to do that. I heard tell of folk who could, but not me."

"You're young," Tesk said. "Perhaps you just needed time." Snowflakes landed on his silver eyelashes as he stared unblinking at Scarlet's hands.

Like Jochi, Tesk was a Setna, but the resemblance ended there. Jochi was reserved; Tesk was a born charmer and probably a libertine in his spare time. Now he was simply fascinated, like all Setna when it came to magic.

Scarlet shook his head. "Maybe." He picked up one of the apples, fearing it would be spoiled or deformed in some way, but it was red and firm. He sniffed it before tucking it into his pocket.

Tesk bent and gathered one as well. "A magic apple." He smiled. "Do you think it will turn me into a toad?"

"Only for a little while." Scarlet chuckled at Tesk's look. "I'm kidding. It's safe enough. Don't blame me if you get a bellyache, though. It might be not be ripe."

"So noted." Tesk lifted his chin and searched the grove. "North?" he suggested.

Scarlet nodded. They changed direction and slipped through the trees for some time, silent as ghosts, senses alert for any movement. The land turned wilder, the trees untrimmed, and the ground uneven. Scarlet stopped in his tracks.

In the lee of a round hill shaded by looming trees was a large animal, not a hundred paces away. A deer, but much bigger than the gangly creatures of the forests of Lysia. It was pale like a snow bear and dotted with sooty spots along its back. The twin antlers were curved in a long, graceful swoop and tipped with wicked points.

At his signal, Tesk sank down to a crouch. The deer snuffled as it buried its nose in a hump of snow and rooted for the lichen hidden beneath.

We're upwind of it, Scarlet realized. Ever so slowly, he raised Whisper, curled his fingers around the bowstring, and pressed into the bow. He closed one eye to take a better aim and waited. He wanted to be sure. He waited so long in the drawn stance that his arm began to shake. Finally, the wind changed and the deer scented them. It lifted its neck—*his* neck—and turned his rump to the hunters with his scut raised, preparing to flee. Scarlet loosed.

The arrow hissed through the air and struck. The buck whistled out a panicked breath and collapsed, his legs kicking.

Tesk released the breath he'd been holding. "Well done!" He grinned. He clapped Scarlet on the shoulder. "Very well done, ser. I wasn't sure you were going to take him. What were you waiting for?"

"I had to be sure he was fair game."

"And how did you find that out? Did the reindeer speak to you? I did not know your magic worked that way."

"It doesn't, but bucks and hinds both grow antlers here. In Lysia, only the bucks have them, and we don't hunt the females in springtime." Scarlet curled his hand like he held something cupped in his palm, and Tesk's jaw dropped.

"You were waiting for sight of his *balls*?"

Scarlet shrugged as Tesk erupted into laughter so loud he knew they wouldn't get near another animal today. They'd probably spooked the game for half a league. He chuckled as Tesk wheezed in mirth and held his sides.

"Want-wit," Scarlet snickered. He laid his bow on the ground and knelt by the spotted reindeer. "He's a big one. Rain-deer did you say?" He slipped the curved hunting knife that Liall had given him from his boot. "Why do you call them that?"

He'd barely grasped the animal's antlers when he heard a sound like hissing steam behind him. He turned and saw nothing, then looked up.

He had never seen an ice cat before. It wasn't much larger than a dog, but it was wiry, the muscles beneath its short gray coat rippling like water. It perched on the branches of the apple tree, black claws dug deep into the wood, sharp ears forward, short tail slashing with fury.

Scarlet froze. There were river cats in Byzantur almost this size, but they were shy, reclusive creatures that fled from all contact with humans. He had never heard of one attacking a person. Not ever.

The ice cat opened its jaws and hissed again, a cloud of mist rushing past twin fangs the size of daggers. Its peaked shoulders tensed to spring. When it moved, it leapt from the branches soundlessly, its gray body matching the color of the clouds against the sky, nearly invisible.

Tesk's arrow took it through the neck in mid-leap. Blood sprayed from the hole, and the graceful leap turned to a screaming, jangled thrashing as it hit the snow.

It had missed Scarlet by the length of one arm.

Blood stained the ice as the cat clawed its way toward him, and Tesk grabbed his shoulder, shoving him back. Scarlet fell out of the way and the cat changed direction, struggling up the hill with the arrow shaft bobbing from its neck. Tesk nocked another arrow and loosed. The cat screamed, shuddered, then was still.

"Deva save us." Scarlet looked wide-eyed at Tesk, knife still in hand.

Tesk's boots stomped up clouds of snow as he strode to him, anger in every muscle. "Hell's teeth! Why didn't you move?"

Scarlet saw that Tesk was shaking. *Not with fear for me, surely.* He swallowed and glanced at the carcass on the hill, curls of steam rising from its blood. "I didn't know it would attack. I thought they were like river cats back home. In Byzantur, no one would believe a cat trying to take down a man."

Tesk slung his bow over his shoulder. "That was *not* a Byzan animal, ser. She was of Rshan. I thought you'd learned by now: every creature in Rshan can be deadly."

Scarlet nodded, staring at the dead cat. Tesk muttered curses in Sinha and helped him up.

On his feet, Scarlet nodded his thanks. "I owe you, friend." He looked at the hill with the cat crowning it. "She'll make a fine pelt anyway."

Tesk didn't seem to be listening. He was looking around at the scraggly apple trees as if they might sprout arms and lunge for them. "We should return to the hunting party now, ser."

"Oh, they'll come running soon enough. You could hear that cat for miles." Scarlet sheathed his knife. He'd be damned if he'd leave without his buck, but Tesk should have something for his trouble, too. He tramped a few steps up the steep hill, his calves disappearing into snow. The ground beneath felt rocky, uneven.

"Ser, get down!" Tesk called in alarm.

For Deva's sake, he was halfway up already! "In a moment. I'm just—"

The hill gave a loud *crack* like an iceberg breaking in half.

Just getting your kill, he thought, then the hill collapsed and the earth gave way, and he was falling past sharpness and rock.

Scarlet felt a burning, tearing pain claw up his leg. His arm was seized and jerked nearly out of its socket. He sucked in a breath of ice crystals and falling earth, but there was not enough air to shout. Stone crashed against his cheek and he was clasped in darkness like a coffin inside a tomb.

The Overworld was not like he imagined.

Scarlet brushed a hanging branch of cedar aside, intent on following a patch of golden light far in the distance. He was in a clearing in a forest, the sun warm on his shoulders. He looked down and saw that he was wearing his red pedlar's coat. It had been months since he took it from the chest. It was patched on the elbows and cuffs, worn and grubby, but it comforted him all the same.

There was music on the wind. Faint, like whispers or birdsong, and not like any music he knew of. The wind smelled like late spring, of flowers and earth.

"Hello?" he called. If it was truly the Overworld, his father should be here to greet him, along with Linhona and all his friends; everyone who had died in Lysia. His chest ached to think of that awful last day, the smell of ashes and rubble, and how empty the world became when he realized his home was gone forever.

Earth is dirt, came Scaja's voice in his ear. *Home is being with the people you love, nothing more.*

He turned and Scaja was there, just like that. "Dad?"

Scaja's smile broke his heart.

"It is you, isn't it?" Scarlet touched Scaja's face with a fingertip, afraid he might vanish like a dream. *But I am dreaming,* he thought.

Scaja clasped him in a bear hug and lifted him off his feet. "There's my wild lad!"

No dream, then. He could scarcely breathe, but he didn't care a bit. Scaja was all right, everyone was all right. He could feel them, all his friends. Old Rufa, who owned the taberna in Lysia. Tommur the baker. Kozi, who had vanished on the Iron Road when they were boys. They were all here!

Except…

Slowly, Scaja let him go. "He's not here, son. Not yet," he said. A wistful smile touched his lined face. "Like you."

"But I am!" Scarlet felt like weeping. "I'm here. You're not a dream."

Scaja ruffled his hair. "Not a dream. Not quite. Things are different where you are. You're closer to the source. You can channel the power for yourself now. Everything you need is at hand."

Channels. Source. Melev had spoken like that. It frightened him.

"Dad?" he said uncertainly.

Scaja faded, like a cloud had passed between them, and Scarlet felt cold steal over his skin.

"What's happening?" he breathed. He reached out, but Scaja was no longer there.

"No," he moaned. "Please come back." *Please don't leave me again.* He smelled jasmine and knew they were in the afarit of Lysia. He could even make out the moon-limned shapes of tombstones in all the grayness.

The Overworld turned brighter. He thought the sun might be coming out, but no. It was snow.

A man approached from a swirling column of snowflakes, as tall as Liall, white-haired, and wearing a red robe. His features were blurred.

The man touched his forehead in a gesture that was oddly familiar, then with two fingers he traced a rune in the air.

Scarlet recognized the rune and recoiled.

"Deva. Om-Ret. Senkhara. The blood of Lyr," the man intoned. The rune seemed to drip fire, and Scarlet could finally see the stranger's eyes. They were gray as steel.

Scarlet shook his head. "I don't understand you. I don't think I want to." Senkhara was a Minh god. That couldn't mean anything good.

"Come to us," the stranger said. "Come to the temple mountain, the place of gods. All your answers are there, and everyone you love. It's all waiting for you, Scarlet."

Again, Melev came to mind. The ancient had wanted more than just magic from him. He had wanted the Creatrix, a powerful instrument of the Shining Ones that had been hidden deep inside a distant mountain. Scarlet knew where that mountain was, but he had told no one except Liall. Liall had refused to speak of it ever again.

But he couldn't mean the Nerit, he thought. It was thousands of leagues away, across the sea.

"The mountain is *here*, Anlyribeth. It waits for you. *She* waits for you."

"Who?" he asked, against all sense and reason. He wanted nothing more than to be away from this man. Why was he lingering to question him? "Who are you?"

"I raised the Black Moat. I saved the realm. I am the *Red King.*"

The very air seemed to turn crimson at the words. A gory curtain swept between them, as if covering the world in blood. And then he was alone, left with the mist and the silence, in a gray space surrounded by a limitless horizon. The taste of metal was in his mouth. He turned, searching for a direction, a sign, anything.

"Scaja?" he called. "Mum?"

But it wasn't Linhona's hand that dragged him from the earth and shook him hard until finally he drew a ragged breath.

Tesk leaned over him, stark fear in his eyes. "Ser! Are you injured? Can you speak?"

He tried to, but the world wavered and blurred, and the last thing he heard was Tesk shouting frantically for aid.

Less Talking

"His arm may be broken, my lord," the curae said.

Liall was coldly furious. He stood with his great arms crossed, his legs planted apart, and glared daggers at the hunting party guards.

The useless hunting party guards, he fumed, knowing no man could command Scarlet, no matter what size. The guardsmen he had assigned to protect his t'aishka were hulking giants even by Rshani standards, well-trained to the sword and the battlefield, and fearless fighters.

And here they stand looking like schoolboys ready for a scolding.

"It's not broken, Liall," Scarlet argued from the bed that he'd been carried to. A livid bruise marked his cheekbone.

Six months in Rshan na Ostre, and Scarlet still refused to call him by his birth name, or even the boyhood diminutive his mother had given him: *Nazir*. Neither would Scarlet accept his own court name: *ser Keriss,* the flame flower. As far as his love was concerned, they were Scarlet the pedlar and Liall the Kasiri bandit, forever.

"My leg is fine, too, whatever your curae tells you." Scarlet's face pinched with lines of pain and he gasped as the curae manipulated the bones of his foot. His snow-pale skin was stained with two bright spots of red high on his cheeks, a sure sign that he was angry as well as injured. "I know when my bones are broken."

These rooms were larger than their old apartments, and far more private—set high in a wing of the outer tier of the palace—but plainer, wide and airy, with great, blue-tinted windows east and west and polished golden boards underfoot. The queen's rooms in the inner tier were too grand and altogether too painful for Liall, and he'd ordered them sealed after her death, wanting to avoid the memories they held.

For himself, Scarlet claimed only a small place in their new chambers: a curtained alcove with a tall window and a fire grate, where he would spend long hours sunk into the deep cushions of the window-seat, perusing the vast library of books in the Nauhinir. It was a new beginning for them, or so Liall had thought.

Today seemed like a replay of old times.

Scarlet's right arm was unwrapped from its bandages and propped with a pillow over his chest. It looked swollen and red, shading to purple in places. His left trouser leg was cut open to the knee, exposing the area where a jagged tree limb had slashed the muscle deep.

Esiuk, the royal curae, took up a needle threaded with boiled sinew and bent over his task. "Please do not move, ser."

"I won't."

Liall wanted to tear the whole palace down. No hunt was without risk. He knew that, and yet despite every precaution he could command, Scarlet had been in danger.

Alexyin had said he would see to placing smaller game in

the grove. Was the lure of easy prey what called the ice cat, or was there something darker at work here?

Tesk was in the room, watching Scarlet with a deep frown. He had saved Scarlet's life, but he didn't seem happy about it, or proud. He seemed angry. "He trusted his weight to a deadfall, sire," he said. "But before, when the cat came, he did not move to protect himself. I think he froze. I beg your forgiveness."

"I was surprised," Scarlet said. "I told you that, Tesk. There's nothing to forgive. It's no one's fault but mine."

Jochi stepped forward tentatively. "Sire?"

Liall turned on him, and the murderous look he gave the Setna stopped him in his tracks. Jochi blushed and began to stammer an apology. Scarlet had remarked that Jochi had the kindest Rshani face he had ever seen, with a gentility that few could appreciate. His tall height was all slenderness and quiet grace, his hair like a length of white silk, and his expressive eyes were a deep gold that hinted at passion.

A passion he has never displayed, Liall thought. *At least not in my sight me. He's always been so coolly polite. The only person he's attached to is Scarlet.*

He cut the air with the flat of his hand, interrupting Jochi's apology and barely missing his nose. "I will not hear excuses from you. Not this time."

"My lord, no one wished him harm. I swear to you—"

"You didn't wish it, but it happened! Is this how you guard my family? You allowed him to leave his guards behind, and so you allowed a dangerous animal within striking distance of him. What if he'd run into a snow bear or a pack of wolves? I have considerable respect for your position and your family, and that's the only reason you're not hanging by your heels over the castle walls. Damn you!" Liall grabbed Jochi by the front of his virca and dragged him close. "Damn your incompetence!"

Scarlet pushed himself up from the bed on his elbow. "Liall, stop!" He hissed in pain and fell back. "Tesk, tell him."

Tesk was silent.

Jochi's expression turned cold. "My lord, if you believe I wish harm to ser Keriss, then I should be hanging over the walls already," he said calmly, though he was up on his tiptoes to keep his balance. "I did try to see you before we left. I wanted more guards; men with hunting skills evenly matched to ser Keriss. I was turned away."

Liall thought back. This morning? He'd been closeted with a Rshani merchant envoy from Sul-na, bringing new trade terms with the Morturii. He barely remembered Jochi's request for an audience.

He uttered a sound of disgust and shoved Jochi away. "I said I would see you later in the day."

Jochi straightened his virca. "Ser Keriss did not wish to hunt later in the day, and he did not wish his game scared off by armored guards clanking through the woods. That's why I wanted the hunters."

"Liall, enough," Scarlet said. He sounded tired.

"Lie down!" Liall shouted. "You're bleeding."

Scarlet roused himself and shouted back. "Stop yelling! The fault was mine. You want to be a bully to someone? Try me."

Despite everything, that brought a smirk to Liall's mouth. Scarlet was the only man in Rshan who dared to speak to him that way. He knew there were rumors that the king was ruled by the small Hilurin like a besotted bride, but those rumors were never uttered to his face. He didn't care anyway. Let them gossip. He had the throne, the power, the army, and he had Scarlet.

They can all go fuck themselves, he thought as he strode to the bed.

"Be quiet and lie down," he ordered. "How bad is it?" he asked Esiuk.

Scarlet narrowed his eyes but reclined on the pillows once more. Liall was not foolish enough to take that as a sign of victory. His ears would be burning from Scarlet's curses later. Scarlet was very fond of Jochi, one of his few true friends in a land not his own.

"The muscle will heal cleanly, my lord," the curae said. "If ser Keriss will hold still long enough for me to finish the stitching, that is."

"You heard him," Liall said. A muscle twitched in his jaw. "Be still and let him work. The rest of you, get out."

Tesk bowed and turned.

"Tesk."

"Sire?"

Liall took Tesk's hand for a moment. "You have my gratitude. I won't forget this service."

Tesk looked down and bowed again formally, almost stiffly. "My king."

With an anguished look at Scarlet, Jochi turned to follow the guards.

Liall's order rang out like a diamond hitting the floor. "Stay, Setna."

Jochi froze. "Yes, my lord." He faced the king.

Scarlet bridled once more, but Liall knew he had put it off too long. It had to be done. He fixed Jochi with a withering look. "For some time you have held the position of tutor and bodyguard to my t'aishka. I intend to relieve you of those duties. If I had a suitable replacement now, I would do it this moment. Until I find a man better suited to the task, I hold you personally responsible for his safety. Is that clear?"

Jochi's golden eyes widened in dismay. "Sire, please."

"Cats stray. Men go where they will," Scarlet spoke up. "He couldn't have known the ice cat would be there, and he isn't responsible for what I do."

Liall kept his attention focused on Jochi. "You are responsible. You will be held responsible. Are we perfectly understood, you and I?" he pressed.

After a brief moment, Jochi shoulder's sagged and he bowed deeply. "Perfectly, sire."

"Good. Now get out."

After Jochi had gone, Liall dragged a chair over to the bed and sat heavily. "Well, say what you have to say."

Scarlet apparently had so much to say that he couldn't decide where to start. He spluttered for a moment in gutter Falx, the language of the Morturii slums, before snarling *bastard* at him and flopping back on his pillows. "Jochi isn't my keeper. I'm a man grown and you can't put my mistakes on him. You have no fucking right!"

"I have every right."

"Just who in Deva's shrieking hell do you think you are?"

"I think I'm the only fucking king in this room." Liall strove for calm. This was not the manner to take with Scarlet. It never worked. He crossed his arms over his chest and leaned back in the chair. "I'm King Nazheradei of Rshan na Ostre, and like it or not, Jochi is my subject and will do as I command."

Scarlet's jaw went tight. "And me?"

"You're Scarlet, son of Scaja the wainwright. You're also ser Keriss *kir* Nazheradei, t'aishka of the king, royal consort, and Lord of the Wild." Liall had formally given Scarlet the noble title last month, along with the Wild itself; a patch of rich hunting lands in the rocky countryside of the Nauhinir. The customary gift of land had angered his court, but it was expected that a nobleman should own something in his own right. It seemed even his small gifts to his t'aishka would be resented. "I don't expect you to obey me, so get your temper down before you burst a vein. What I do expect is for you not to openly curse me or to coax my servants and vassals to defiance. What do you think would happen to Jochi if you were killed?"

Scarlet frowned. "You wouldn't do that."

Liall snorted. "Don't wager on it. Living as atya of the Kasiri is not so far away in my memory, and krait-law is not that different from Rshani law. I would have made him pay for your life, and your guards would have paid as well. Is that what you want?"

Reminding Scarlet of their Byzantur adventuring seemed to get through, because his chin dropped. "Of course not. Now that there's light to see, I only wanted to wander a bit and taste more of the land. You said hunting was safe."

So that was it. Scarlet's wilding nature was coming to life with the sun. "Hunting is never safe. I said it was *safer* within the palace grounds, not outside of them, as you well know." Liall sighed. "We have not spent much time together lately, I know. That's why I leave you in Jochi's company: because you're fond of him and he cares for you. He would not allow you to come to harm. That is, if he can help it." He cupped Scarlet's face in both his big hands, making Scarlet look at him. "You outrank him, love. Jochi has to obey you the same as he must obey me. He tried to change your mind about going off alone with Tesk. I know he did."

When Scarlet did not protest, Liall went on. "He *tried* to change your mind. And when that didn't work, he bowed to your will, *as he must,* and obeyed. You left him no other avenue."

"I'm sick of being watched and followed like a thief. It's not my way to have eyes on me all the time."

"It's unwise for a king's t'aishka to go traipsing through the woods alone—"

"I don't *traipse!*"

"Because," Liall continued, "quite apart from all the ordinary dangers, you make a very tempting target for my enemies." His thumb brushed the curving mark under

Scarlet's right eye. A mariner had dealt that wound. It was faded in color, but the scar would remain gray, as if someone had drawn a fine line there in ashes. Hilurin always scarred so.

"I wanted to kill the man who did this to you, remember? I haven't exactly kept my love for you a secret. At first, it didn't matter, because Cestimir was to be king and we were supposed to leave. You're my weakness, Scarlet, and now everyone knows it." He kissed Scarlet on the forehead, then sat back and looked at him steadily. "And you cannot go anywhere alone, love. Not anymore. Not as long as I'm king. I never intended to bring you here at all, but now that you are here and—I hope—intend to remain, our lives must change." He massaged the bridge of his nose tiredly. "I thought we'd covered this ground already."

"We have," Scarlet said morosely.

"And so?"

Scarlet shrugged. "As you say, you've been busy. We've spent little time together in the past month. I wanted a change. I got bored."

Liall grunted. *And grew tired of having palace gossip poured into your ears.* "Deva save us all from a bored Hilurin."

Scarlet winced as Esiuk's needle threaded through his skin. "I took down a buck before I fell."

"A reindeer?" Liall couldn't stop himself from grinning. "With your little bow? You amaze me. Is there anything you can't do?"

"Fly, for one." Scarlet shook his head. "I thought it was a hill made of earth or an outcropping of rock. It didn't look like a deadfall. Even if it was, I expected the ice would hold me up."

"The ice becomes rotten this time of year, especially so close to the sea. Any area off the main paths can be treacherous. Did you enjoy using the bow?" Liall was glad to be off the topic of his many absences and glad that they were not snapping at each other anymore. Scarlet's temper was like quicksilver, but so was his forgiveness. He never stayed cross for long, and for that Liall was grateful. Lately, though, gossip of Ressilka had put a wedge between them, and Liall ached to see it gone.

Scarlet nodded. "The bow is a fine way to hunt. Better than snaring, anyhow, and surer."

Deer and other game in Scarlet's homeland were brought down by snares, spears, traps, or staked pits. In Byzantur and even Morturii, the bow was a cowardly weapon of disgrace, the tool of assassins and spies. Any weapon that put a man beyond arm's reach was shameful to use, and even possessing one with the excuse of hunting was extremely dangerous. A bow was an indictment, and the man who owned one could be accused of many things. Scarlet had never even touched a bow before coming to Rshan.

"I'm glad you've taken to the weapon. It's a pretty thing, is it not?" Liall glanced at the door where Scarlet's heavy hunting cloak and boots had been piled, the slender bow named *Whisper* resting on top of them. A servant would put them away later, when they judged it prudent to return.

Scarlet followed Liall's gaze. The supple bow was carved from seasoned black oak, the grip inlaid with bone and silver and mother of pearl fittings in the swirling Ostre Sul pattern of the winter aurora. Though it was perfect for Scarlet, it was half the size of a Rshani bow and a fourth of the drawing power. Liall had known it would be good for hunting rabbits and small game, but with accuracy and swiftness, an arrow was deadly to a target of any size. A rabbit was smaller than a man's head, after all, and an eye makes a handy target. It pleased him to know that he had added one more defense to Scarlet's arsenal.

"Very pretty," Scarlet agreed. "I'm getting better, but some of my arrows still go wide of my mark."

"The bow is yours, but no man owns the arrow, Scarlet." Liall was suddenly serious. "Remember that. An arrow can always go astray, even at the last moment. No man ever masters it completely."

"What about women? I bet Jarek would be a fair shot with my lady there. I still feel strange picking her up, like I should be looking over my shoulder for an Ankarian guard to call me out as a spy."

"She?" Liall chuckled. "You think your bow a female, then? My t'aishka finally decides to sample the pleasures of a woman, but she's made of wood."

That tugged an embarrassed smile from Scarlet, despite Esiuk's presence. "As if I'd ever. Even if I liked her, I wouldn't know what to do. I'd make a mess of it, that's for sure." He shook his head. "Things are so different here. You have masters but no slaves, magic but no gods, and men can lie with men, and women with women, and no one takes the slightest notice."

"You're the only magic this country has seen in a thousand years." Liall ignored the remark about men. Scarlet was not ashamed to be known as his lover, but the stigmas inflicted on Scarlet in his homeland were hard to erase. Liall hoped that, in time, he would completely forget them.

He is young. Time will erase those memories, and he will forget that he ever lived in a country that killed men such as him, or put brands of shame on their flesh.

Scarlet scratched his palm idly. "I think my magic is stronger, here. Is that possible? It must be the cold or somesuch. I swear, my hands felt like they wanted to kindle a fire withy when I fell through the deadfall. That wouldn't have been good."

Liall went cold at the sudden mental image of Scarlet surrounded by the rotten wood of the deadfall and wreathed in fire.

Esiuk glanced up, his attention pulled from his task by talk of magic. Every curae Liall had ever known was intensely curious about such things. Esiuk was a loyal retainer, but in learned men, the thirst for knowledge was boundless and unpredictable.

"It must have been the fear," Liall said quickly. "You were frightened."

"Not that much."

Liall didn't want to dwell on the subject, especially not with Esiuk listening. He had trusted Melev once, too. "Well, it's over now and you're here, if only a little worse for wear. Nothing broken and now you're warm and safe. But are you quite finished turning the castle upside-down for the rest of the week?"

Scarlet suddenly looked wary. "Why do you ask that?"

"I may have to be away for a time."

Scarlet's expression turned from cautious to blank. "Oh?"

"Yes. It won't be for very long, I promise." *Just as long as it takes to win a war. The barons are already gathered, all the pawns in one palace, and no queen; just a new king to risk his crown and his head.*

"I see."

And just that. No questions, no protests. The painful and distant wedge growing between them widened. Liall had known from the beginning that their months in Rshan might turn into years, but that was when Cestimir was the heir, and they never expected to remain here forever. After the coronation, Liall had let himself believe that once Scarlet got a feel for the court and his position, he would be happy here. It was no shock to Liall that a reserved Hilurin youth raised in the rustic Byzantur countryside would flounder in the opulence of a royal court, but simply hoping it would get easier with time was wishful thinking. Scarlet had seemed content for a while, but then the rumors about Ressilka had sprouted like weeds. Now there were Rshani who had reasons other than bigotry to make Scarlet feel unwelcome.

I will keep him with me, Liall thought fiercely. *No matter what the cost. If all of Rshan, my people, and my birthright must be hung 'round my neck, so be it, but Scarlet is mine. I will not lose this one happiness.*

He looked at Esiuk's hands as the curae deftly finished sewing the lacerated skin of Scarlet's calf. "Does it hurt much?"

Scarlet flinched as the needle pushed in and out of his skin. His voice was neutral. "Cuts and bruises. I've had worse.

It's nothing."

Liall's heart sank. *It's a great deal to me*, he thought. *You could have been killed. I'd have lost you forever. Why don't you ask where I'm going? I'd prefer a fight to this.*

"This will leave a scar, sire," Esiuk spoke up. The round dome of his head, shaved smoothly bald like all Rshani physicians, gleamed in the lamplight.

"If it does, you'll have one to match," Liall said.

"Don't listen to him," Scarlet said.

Liall merely raised a snow-white eyebrow and regarded Scarlet in silence. The quiet remained until Esiuk had bandaged Scarlet's leg with clean linen.

"Will you be wanting a draught for the pain, ser?" Esiuk inquired.

Scarlet shook his head. "I'll set a withy to it on my own. Thank you, ser."

Esiuk gave him an intense stare, and Liall knew that the curae would have desperately liked to see the withy chant in action, but dared not ask. Esiuk packed his tools and left.

When they were truly alone, Liall rose slowly from his chair and stood looking down at the young man to whom he had bound his life and his heart.

"I thought Tesk and Jochi were friends," Scarlet said. "Why didn't Tesk speak up for him?"

"Because it was Jochi's mistake. Tesk was there, Jochi wasn't. Imagine if you'd insisted on going alone into the grove."

Scarlet looked a bit too pleased with himself. "So it *was* my fault, just as I said."

"I'll allow that your stubbornness is partly to blame, yes," Liall said. "But one truth has become very clear to me: your nature requires a bodyguard with vastly more skill, one who can tiptoe around your damned Hilurin obstinacy and still be a sword between you and danger."

"Oh." Scarlet rolled his eyes. "I pity this man already."

"Save the pity for me. A village peasant pedlar putting the high king of Rshan in his place. Don't think I don't know how much you enjoy it."

Scarlet had the grace to smirk. "Well… I never think of you as *the king*. Whenever I get the better of you, I always imagine it's Liall of the Kasiri I'm putting on his arse."

"For charging you too stiff a toll to cross his mountain, no doubt." Liall carefully slid into the bed beside Scarlet and drew a hand through his black hair, mindful of his injuries.

"Tch, it was never *your* mountain. I had more claim to the Nerit than ever you did."

"I had warriors."

"Brawlers, more like." Scarlet shifted closer to him. "Now, your Rshani, those are warriors. Never seen men fight so well or so…" He hesitated, searching for a word.

"Single-mindedly," Liall supplied. He traced a careful finger down the cloth bindings on Scarlet's arm.

"I suppose that must be the word. Or two words, because your lot never says five words when they can say the same thing in twenty."

"It's the long winters. Boredom sets in and must have an outlet of some fashion."

"Whatever that means. You're a funny old bunch, no doubt. But I think I got the better deal with you."

Liall chuckled and pulled Scarlet carefully to lie against his chest. He pressed his nose into Scarlet's hair to inhale the scent of him. "You do? I'm flattered," he said, his voice muffled. "That's as close as you've ever gotten to true praise for your king."

"You ent my king."

"Aren't. Are not." Liall pulled back and tilted Scarlet's chin up to him. He brushed his lips searchingly over Scarlet's smooth and hairless cheek, careful of the bruises.

"Yes, that's what I said."

He found Scarlet's mouth and there was no more talking for a while.

The hour came while Scarlet was still curled warm around him. A hand shook Liall's shoulder, and he squinted and cursed until he saw it was Nenos.

Liall sighed. "Oh… yes. It's today, isn't it?"

Nenos bowed. "Yes, lord," he whispered, always careful not to disturb Scarlet, who woke anyway. "Your bath is waiting."

Scarlet rolled over and flapped a hand at Liall. "Go," he

muttered, pulling the blankets over his head.

Liall got up, stretched, and padded naked to the door.

"Robe," Scarlet called, muffled under the covers.

Nenos offered a heavy robe and Liall wrapped it awkwardly around his waist, holding it up with his hands. If Scarlet could make the effort to learn Rshani customs, Liall could keep some of the Hilurin ones. In Scarlet's village, there was a place for nudity and with very few exceptions that place was either the bed or the washing tub.

They had both made enough compromises for each other to know which customs were negotiable and which were not. This one was not.

Chos waited kneeling by the sunken bath, stripped to the waist and nearly obscured by a cloud of steam. He bowed his neck when Liall entered. "Good morning, my lord. I hope you slept well?"

A sharp scent infused the chamber as the cedar panels lining the walls bled their aroma. Still groggy, Liall grunted a reply, let the robe fall, and stepped down into the water. He lowered himself to the waist in the great marble basin and splashed his face before feeling for a seat on the submerged bench. Chos took up the soap and a rough cloth and reached for his shoulders.

When his back was scrubbed clean, Liall thanked Chos and dismissed him.

"Are you sure, my lord? Who will shave you?"

He scraped his hair back from his forehead, feeling the stubble on his chin. "Nenos can do that. Go along, boy, I can manage."

Chos had a round face (*like a full moon*, Scarlet had remarked) and a thin mouth that suddenly pinched in disagreement. "But your bath is not finished, sire."

"I'll finish it on my own." Liall stared at the servant when he did not leave. "Am I unaware of some problem?"

Chos bent his neck again. "Of course not. Please excuse me, my lord." He got to his feet and made a hasty exit.

Now what was that about? There were twenty attendants assigned to the wing, efficient shadows who made every aspect of his personal household from meals to laundry seem effortless. Nenos had selected Chos and three other attendants from their old apartments. Of them all, Chos was the least qualified and the most conspicuous about simply *being* there.

It was not that Chos was ill-mannered. Quite the opposite, really. He was too courteous, too eager to draw attention to his presence. If he aspired to become a retainer, he would have to learn that his place was not at the center of the room, but in the background.

Nenos was responsible for Chos's training, which the young man would need if he wanted the freedom to decide where he would be employed and for how much. Many times Liall had overheard Nenos quietly instructing him in table settings, household manners, linens and silver, how to deftly turn away a caller from the door; skills that could be parlayed into a valuable position with a noble house. He wondered if Nenos had some attachment to Chos, or if they were kinsmen. That would explain much.

"I have other problems than the moods of silly servant boys," he muttered, and dunked his head under the water.

When he was dried, shaven, and laced into a plain virca, he sent for Alexyin.

"I hope I'm doing the right thing," Liall said.

Alexyin held the door open for him. "So do I, my lord."

They began the long walk to the great hall. Save for the guards posted at intervals along the corridors, they were alone.

Alexyin glanced pointedly at Liall's necklace. "Two common coins? An odd token for a ruler to wear," he remarked.

Liall's necklace was a length of leather cord holding a pair of copper coins with a square hole stamped in the middle of each. He tucked it away into the collar of his virca. "It's not a token, but a reminder."

"What does my king need reminding of?"

That my pride is a blindness, he thought. But that would take too much explanation and it was not a memory he wanted to share. Scarlet had given him the coins as toll to travel the mountain road where they met. Liall kept them as a symbol of everything that had happened after that meeting and everything he had learned from it, mostly from Scarlet. The humble necklace was now one of his most precious possessions.

"That I'm never as clever as I pretend to be," he improvised. "If I'm wrong this time, it won't be bearskins decorating the palace, but my own hide and probably yours, too. After the murder of their rightful prince and the execution of their *spare* prince, I fear many believe that the Kinslayer has come home only to finish the job. The rebellion in Magur was bad enough. We can't afford another."

"Spare prince," Alexyin repeated with emphasis. "You never mention Vladei in my presence unless you're forced to, my lord. Or the Lady Shikhoza."

Shikhoza had wed Vladei's brother, Eleferi, only a few days after Cestimir's interment at the Kingsdal. There had been no funeral for Vladei, nor any mourning. Liall had forbidden it.

"Astute observation. What of it?"

"Nothing, sire, except that if I notice it, others eventually will."

And wonder at the omission. He glanced at the cold lines of Alexyin's profile. "Does Ressanda truly believe I crossed the waters of the Norl Ūhn simply to take revenge on my family?"

"A loyal subject would never think such a thing."

"Loyalty," Liall stated, "is a matter of perspective. One man's fealty could be another's treason. A kingdom divided needs a common threat to unite it, an enemy that all can all agree on. One just happens to be at our gates."

"The Ava Thule," Alexyin said.

"The Ava Thule," Liall echoed. "Don't say it like they're a particularly clever figment of my imagination. The threat is very real."

For many decades, the Ava Thule tribesmen had attacked small villages and towns on the borders of Nau Karmun. Once they had what they wanted—women, food, supplies, and slaves—they vanished again. Vladei had bribed the Ava Thule to swell the ranks of his red guards during the rebellion in Magur, promising the savages rich lands, coin, women, whatever they wished. Before that, the tribesmen had never dared attack a major city. When challenged in force, the Ava Thule way was to retreat deeper into the Tribelands. If pressed, they would go much further, into a hellish place where only Ancients and rift creatures could survive. Somehow, Vladei had been able to cajole thousands of them to join his cause.

"We thinned them out in Magur," Alexyin said.

"Not thin enough. No matter how many campaigns we wage, they come back. Like lice."

"Alas for the poor lice of Magur."

Liall's brows drew together. "I was disturbed to hear the reports of slaughter that occurred there, but I did not order it. My lady mother did."

"Is that to be her legacy? Her last act as queen was to murder a city and burn the populace in their beds?"

"No," Liall snapped. Then, quieter: "No. Let them blame me if they will. It might even work to our advantage in the end. All the world fears a butcher, and we need Uzna Minor and her gentle baroness to support us."

"Don't you mean the baron?"

Liall smirked. Eleferi was as much a baron as Alexyin was a dancing master. "What, the little man who kindly offered his balls to Shikhoza along with his wedding ring? My silk-swaddled step-brother would dice, drink, and whore his way through ten lifetimes rather than spend a single moment running his barony. That's what he has Shikhoza for."

"Among other purposes. I've heard rumor that the baroness and her husband share a lover."

Liall's eyebrows went up a notch. "Your ears hear more than mine, then. Who is he?"

"Some disgraced Setna, young enough that I blush to tell you his age. And the tales I've heard of his carousing..." Alexyin shook his head. "Though a boy, he's a libertine to put Eleferi to shame."

"That's quite an accomplishment, knowing Eleferi. And you say Shikhoza beds this rogue?" Liall was amazed. "She's changed."

They arrived at the doors. A female guard with a starred blue badge of rank on her shoulder bowed and stepped aside.

Liall signaled for the doors to be opened. "Come, friend. Let's turn our minds from one pack of whores to the next."

Those who saw the king enter the vaulted chamber of the great hall did so to the sound of Alexyin's laughter. The low hum and buzzing of voices ceased.

Theor, the king's equerry and new Master of Horse, stood with axe in hand. The man was a celebrated warrior with a square chin like a block of stone, a white beard, and a chest as broad as a bull.

Theor's rich voice boomed throughout the hall: *"Nazheradei, blood prince of the Camira-Druz, master of the North Sea, Baron of Sul, Baron of Nau Karmun, Prince of the Kalaxes Isles, and Rightful King of Rshan na Ostre!"*

The crowd parted smoothly and bowed low. Liall swept past them, wondering how many of the assembled found Theor's proclamation as pompous as he did. Alexyin followed him to the dais.

Tesk was present. The man had an obvious manner for a spy, always prating of paintings and art, his perfume announcing him louder than even Theor could have managed. Such a peacock's mask would fool most, but not everyone.

Still, Tesk had saved Scarlet. Such a service could not be forgotten.

The high, domed blue ceiling was dotted with gold and silver in the patterns of the stars, the Longwalker constellation glittering in crystal and silver directly above the carved wooden platform of the king's dais. An enormous casement window in the north wall was thrown open to reveal the land spreading out below the heights of the Nauhinir, and the walls were lined with panels of silk tapestries and the banners of noble houses.

A small lacquered chest rested on a table on the dais.

As he mounted the steps, Liall was keenly aware that he did so alone. None of the western barons were present themselves, even though Uzna Minor and Sul were far closer to the Nauhinir than far-flung eastern holdings like Tebet. Liall had at least expected baronial emissaries from Jadizek, but though the baron of Jadizek was the crown's staunchest eastern ally, none had arrived. All those gathered in the hall were lesser nobles, equerries, secretaries, and the poor relations of nobility sent to listen and report. And Tesk, of course, whose yellow silk virca flashed with brilliant embroidered birds.

There are no teeth in this hall, Liall thought. Whatever he decided, it was obvious that no one wanted to share the responsibility and the resulting blame—or even glory— that might follow. As a Kasiri atya, he had wielded absolute power over his krait, the final word in all disputes. In Rshan, control of the sprawling continent was parceled out to the barons, to govern as the king's vassal-princes under his justice. But it was still a monarchy, and whether here in the chambers or in the yurts of the krait, both the burden and the blame would fall to him alone.

He was surprised that being the Wolf of Omara and being king of Rshan could feel so similar. *My old wolf fangs will have to serve me today.*

He looked down on the milling crowd and raised his arm to show them his palm. At once, all eyes were on him.

"Last year, in the months before my return to Rshan, there was a revolt in Magur," Liall said, pitching his deep voice to reach all corners of the room. "Vladei's rebellion was his final, failed bid to become king. It was a treasonous plot that cost Prince Cestimir his life. Most of you know that there were reports of Ava Thule fighting alongside those rebels. We thought there were only a handful of tribal warriors in Magur, perhaps a few hundred at most." He paused. "I have been informed that during the revolt, Vladei paid Tribesmen to cross the Greatrift in the thousands."

Alexyin stood just below the dais. He shot Liall a look of caution as the chamber buzzed like a kicked beehive.

Liall rapped his knuckles on the wood of the dais for

quiet.

"You should have put a sword through every living thing in Magur!" a man shouted. "Spit them like mad dogs! Hang them from the trees and put the entire city to the torch!"

"And then shall I command my army to spit infants on lances like Ramung did in the black years?" Liall scorned. The man wore the purple colors of Tebet, but Liall did not recognize his face. "I am not Ramung. So long as I am king we will not butcher women and children for the crime of being in the wrong place, or having the wrong fathers or husbands. And the city *was* put to the torch. Khatai Jarek assures me that every man who bore arms against us was killed in battle, incinerated, or executed afterward."

"Every *man,*" the Tebeti stressed. "Not every male. Was it Queen Nadiushka who spared the young boys and allowed the animals to take root and flourish in our midst, or was it you, sire?"

Liall looked down on him. The man had a sharp face and a reddish tint to the thin, pointed beard he sported. Liall fancied he had the look of a young Baron Ressanda. "Who are you, ser?"

"Jarad Hallin, of Tebet."

Hallin meant *drover*. It was a new name, not claimed by any of the noble houses of Rshan. From the look of Hallin, he had Morturii blood somewhere in his ancestry. No few did these days, especially in Tebet.

"*Ser* Hallin," Liall said with an edge of mockery in his voice. There were scattered titters throughout the room, and for once the customary prejudice of his people was something he could make use of. Few nobles would want to be seen allying with the political views of a peasant. "It is true that Jarek pardoned the youths who joined their fathers in revolt, so long as they swore an oath never to take up arms against the crown again. Those who would not swear—and there were no few—were beheaded."

"Their *word*," Hallin sneered. "And what good is the word of a fatherless rebel bastard?"

"Almost as good as the word of a cow-herder," Liall replied.

Hallin's expression turned sullen as chuckles scurried through the hall like a nasty rumor, and Liall knew he had won. A distasteful victory, but he would take it.

"The men of Magur have paid," he said, raising his voice one more. "When the battle was lost, the Ava Thule fled like the cowards they, but not to the Tribelands. They are still here."

While the crowd erupted into shouts and calls, Alexyin moved quickly to join him on the dais. Alexyin shot a look at the lacquered chest, only now seeming to notice the brilliant blue of the varnish, and the royal badge of stars set in diamond on the lid. Liall saw that Alexyin knew what it meant, and that he was not pleased.

"Sire," Alexyin said into Liall's ear, "you will lose the advantage if you reveal everything now."

"I don't agree," Liall answered, keeping his head down and his face turned into Alexyin's shoulder in case there were lip-readers in the chamber. *He chooses this moment to have an opinion?* he thought. His mentor had been painfully distant on the matter of the proposed war, close-mouthed to the point of insolence at times. Now Alexyin wanted to be heard. Why now?

"This information would be useful as bait," Alexyin argued.

"Some secrets are more damaging if they're kept, and ultimately a member of *my* family is responsible for this invasion," Liall said. "Dead or not, it makes no difference. I am Camira-Druz and the blame will fall to me."

"I could watch to see who lets this secret slip. How else would they know unless they were allied with *them?* The death of your enemies is better than the goodwill of your friends."

An astute observation, but one that led to a ruthless path. Liall shook his head. "I will not be that kind of ruler. We'll need more than friends to drive the Ava Thule out of our lands for good. We'll need the whole kingdom."

"I don't agree."

"It's not your decision."

Alexyin pursed his mouth crossly and rapped his fist on the table. The noise died down. "The king shall speak!"

Liall scanned the faces of the crowd, meeting an attentive eye here, a dagger-look there. He had many friends, he saw, but there were many more he could not read. Currents ran around him like the rushing of a stream. *It will become a river soon enough, and much will be swept away. Time for the king's famous speech, where he stirs the soldiers to courage before the battle, except this is a Rshani battle, and nothing ever goes like in the stories.*

He was not looking forward to that part.

"On my lady mother's command, soldiers under Khatai Jarek were sent to garrison Magur after the battle, but the soldiers will not remain there. They will be recalled to Starhold." Liall looked quickly around the room to see who understood and who did not, and was pleased to see that many men in attendance were no fools. He nodded. "For centuries, the Ava Thule have attacked from the shadows, killing our men, stealing our women, kidnapping our children into their twisted litters to corrupt their hearts. We will rout these vermin from their holes and drag them into the sun to die on our pikes." His gaze raked the crowd. "They have taken the hills beneath Ged Fanorl."

Ged Fanorl. The sacred mountain of the Shining Ones, forbidden to men.

The previous noise was nothing to the roar that spilled out of the chamber and into the halls. Shouts of derision, fear, excitement, and accusation echoed around him:

"Blasphemy! Kill the defilers!"

"All lies! There is no threat!"

"Magur was sacrificed for the warmongers!"

"The filthy tribesmen will be slaughtering us on the streets of Sul next! They will fire the ships in the harbor and feast on our flesh!"

Liall closed his ears to the ruckus. It reminded him of the same paranoia and disbelief over Scarlet's magic: that it was either a myth or it existed only to destroy them. Months had passed and the prophesied Hilurin Doom had not come. Instead, Scarlet's beauty, wit, and bravery had gained him dozens of admirers.

With time and a little luck, Scarlet might even begin to

think of Rshan as his home.

The king remained on the dais with Alexyin and let the chamber thrash it out. By custom, he had no voice when they argued among themselves, and the usual court etiquette was ignored. If a man was invited to council, he was allowed to say what was on his mind, even to the king. Creative insults were not uncommon. Scarlet would have been greatly shocked.

Liall crossed his arms. "In Byzantur," he said aside to Alexyin, "no commoner is allowed to look on the face of the Flower Prince. And in Morturii, they revere their king so deeply that no man, common or noble, is permitted to raise their voice to him."

"We could use a bit of that today," Alexyin grumbled at the noisy crowd. "They're like a brood of clucking hens spying a fox."

"If they don't stop, fetch a bucket of water."

Alexyin grunted. "A few spears would serve better."

"None of that," Liall warned. "We have foxes aplenty among us, but the nobles are more useful alive than dead. Any man—indeed every man—can be forced to agree, but we want to win minds here, not just swords. If I wanted the barons dead, that's done easily enough. I need the full support of the nobles, in spirit as well as word, and my kingdom needs to be free of this endless dissent and fear. I was raised with royal plotting and treachery, but I do not intend to live the rest of my life that way."

"Dead foxes can still be put to use. My neck is better warmed by a collar of fur."

Astute and ruthless again, and he's not entirely wrong. "I wonder if it is not the color that entices you."

Alexyin lifted a snow-white eyebrow and his mouth curved. "A red fox?" He chuckled with real humor.

Ressanda had declined to attend the council. Instead, the baron had sent the ill-bred Jarad Hallin as emissary, an insult if Liall ever saw one.

Liall promised himself that he would fully attend to the matter of Ressanda soon, so that many other worries could be laid to rest. Ressanda wanted a royal husband for his daughter, but Cestimir's body was long cold. The baron looked now to more promising prospects.

I fear he will not take no for an answer. But how can I break Scarlet's heart to honor a promise only half made?

"My lord! My lord king!" A courtier waved his arms from the crowd, vying with many others in the sea of voices.

"I will not speak to a mob, ser," Liall answered, pitching his voice to be heard.

Theor's beard quivered as he clenched his lantern jaw. "Silence! Can't you see the king is waiting? Stop your wailing! *Shut it, ya squeaking bastards!*" His booming voice crashed over the heads of the petty nobles like a thunderclap. He leaned easily on his axe and nodded at Liall. "The king wants to talk."

"We will not tolerate this blasphemy," Liall said. "I have sent Khatai Jarek to Sul, there to conscript new recruits and to forage and supply for a campaign."

A rousing shout went up, but there were still many voices of dissent mingled with questions:

"What of the Ancients? Ged Fanorl belongs to them! Let the Ancients deal with them!"

"What about my lord's holdings to the north, his lands and fields?"

"My baron had farms and flocks in Magur! What of them?"

"To hell with your fields! What about the coin we sent to lure workers back to that blasted place? Where did that go?"

Liall nodded to Theor, who bellowed again for quiet. When he had their attention, he went to the table and opened the lacquered chest. He took an object from it, holding it high for all to see, wondering how many would recognize it.

A deep hush fell over the chamber.

He turned the dagger in his fingers. It was small, no larger than his hand, with a thin blade and a rounded pommel. The blade itself was a mixture of vivid crimson and muddy black, like a fresh wound.

"Blood steel," he said loudly, letting the power of his voice, trained from childhood to tones of command, roll over the watchers. "There is no other metal like this in all of Nemerl. Long ago, we lost the alchemy to forge it. This weapon was taken from the body of a dead Ava Thule in Magur. It comes from *inside* the temple mountain, from holy Ged Fanorl itself. The Ava Thule have defiled it and stolen from the Shining Ones, who are the makers of us all." He slammed the dagger point-down into the table. The metal flared bright for an instant and sang with a metallic whine as it sheared through the hard wood, buried to the hilt.

Theor raised his axe. *"DEATH!"* he roared. *"Death to Ava Thule!"*

The call was taken up until the hall rang with a hundred voices, a sea of raised fists and open mouths shouting *Death!*

Alexyin flipped his long braid away from his shoulder. His eyes were hooded. "Well, you've got your war."

Tesk was to bring the new man to Liall's private solar. Liall sat with the table between himself and the door, a flagon of cold wine and two cups waiting.

Ged Fanorl, he thought, and wondered what the hall made of his performance. He wasn't good at acting, or at pretending shock or outrage.

No, your lies take a different talent.

The sacred mountain had been violated long ago, even before his exile. Only a few knew that secret, and those few had high stakes in protecting the knowledge. Captain Qixa would surely be put to death, and the others…

His mouth twisted and he was busy damning himself to three different hells when the door opened and Tesk entered. A lean man shadowed him.

Liall's first impression of Margun Rook was that the man was like the ragged remnants of a once-fine garment. He could discern the nobility in Margun's high brows and his straight, narrow nose, and a sober intelligence in his deep-set eyes, but his muscular arms bore many scars of battle. The marks were smooth and thin, obviously made by sharp steel. Another razor-thin scar circled his left eye socket like a crescent moon, the end trailing down his cheek. *A knife,* Liall thought. *Not by chance, either. That was done with care.*

Margun's white hair was crowned with a widow's peak that framed his face in two streaks of smoky gray, long enough to brush his shoulders. He wore a brown, sleeveless virca with the serpent badge of a Setna on his breast.

"Thank you, Tesk," Liall said.

"My lord." Tesk put his hand over his heart and performed one of his elegant bows. The look he shot Margun was anything but graceful. "Remember my words," he warned, and left them.

Unlike solariums—which were rooms constructed solely to gather and channel light—solars were rather small palace rooms with a single wall of glass. This one was a wide, airy gable with walls unrelieved by tapestries or banners. A curving wall of thick, milky glass faced the east. It was a room for seeing, and Liall liked to conduct his interviews here, where shadows could not hide.

He studied Margun for several moments as the man waited at attention, his gaze fixed straight ahead. Liall noted that his eyes were the color of blue slate, but the next moment they seemed to be darker, the color of flint.

Changeable eyes, he thought. A chameleon of a man.

"Margun Rook," he said, leaning back in his chair. "What words did Tesk have for you?"

"Words." Margun's voice was low and deep, with a hint of northern lilt. "They were not precisely… words."

Threats, then. Well done, Tesk. "You hail from noble stock. I've heard the tale of Margun Siran, Ramung's chief assassin in the days of my great-grandfather."

Margun clasped his hands behind his back. "We are who we are, my lord."

"True enough. I don't remember your face from the campaigns, but I remember hearing your name."

Margun did not react, and Liall was not pleased. *He can't think I'll trust him, can he?*

But Tesk had found Margun and Alexyin vouched for him. That had to mean something. Liall tried a new tack. "Tell me why you decided to betray your commander."

Margun's eyes flickered. "I do not believe I betrayed my oath, sire. I only held myself truer to it."

"By refusing to follow orders, inciting your brother-soldiers to defect and lay down their arms? I spent my youth being schooled in the language of nuance, but it will take more than a clever turn of phrase to convince me that direct defiance of a superior is *not* insubordination."

"It was a bad war," Margun answered straightly. "The Tribelands were your first campaign, my lord, but not mine. What happened there was… it was not right. Conquerors should be better rulers than what was done to the north. I will do what I must to defend my family, my country, and my king, but some orders should never be given."

"If every common soldier felt free to question the orders of their commanders, there would be no wars fought at all."

A ghost of a smile touched the wide, hard line of Margun's mouth. "Yes, sire. That's quite true."

Liall gave a short hum of thought. "You were in

command of a cohort of men under Khatai Jarek. You refused a direct order to put a village to the sword, and the next month the village you so benevolently spared joined with the Ava Thule and put a third of the smallholder farms in Uzna Minor to the torch, along with the farmers. Do I have that correct? Your life was spared and you were sent to the Setna to learn better sense. Well? Have you learned anything?"

"Sixty-three years is a long time, my lord. I learned many things, among them the fact that a man must answer ultimately to himself alone. I may not have been wise in my decision to spare the village, but I was true to my conscience and their blood is not on my hands. I could not have done it and stayed myself. And yet, I failed my people and my queen when I refused to obey." Margun shrugged. "Just as many died from my refusal as would have died from my compliance. I was not a good soldier. I was lucky to be sent to the Setna."

"You were lucky to keep your head. I'd have taken it. If you're a man who courts his doubts, please don't doubt that one. I'd have executed you quickly, so you wouldn't have had time to interrogate that sensitive conscience of yours."

Margun bent his head. "I didn't mean to offend you, sire."

"When you offend me, you'll know it."

"Yes, sire."

I keep trying to put him off-balance and it isn't working, Liall thought. Perhaps that was a good sign. "I don't need a mindless brute to keep my t'aishka safe. I want a man who thinks for himself, but not one who thinks so much that he ponders disobedience in favor of his own mind. I don't know you, but Tesk does. Alexyin says you're up to the task, and I trust his judgment."

Margun nodded his head slowly. "But," he said.

Liall waited. When it became apparent that Margun would speak no more, the king smiled thinly. "But trusting Alexyin is not the same as trusting you. While he believes you'd make a fine guard for Scarlet, Alexyin's notion of what Scarlet needs and my own differ greatly. Have you ever known a Hilurin?"

Margun's eyebrows went up. "No. None. Should I have?"

"I've been informed that you've never traveled outside of Rshan, so no. Definitely not. And there lies the problem."

Margun frowned and shifted on his feet, his boots scuffling on the floor. "Because they are so different from us?"

"I did not say that. They are actually very like us, but how you might expect a Hilurin to act and how one might truly behave are two different things. When I first traveled south as young man, I landed in Volkovoi. I saw a few faces in the city that reminded me of home, so I stayed." He paused. "It was one of the worst choices I ever made. Volkovoi is full of the worst sort of cutthroats, as well as thieves, pirates, smugglers, whores, and Minh. But because of those men, the ones who look like us and reminded me of home, I stayed. I learned that the city employed men of Northern blood as guards, and for good pay, too. Bravos, they're called. I thought they might be like our own people, so I joined them." Liall paused to sip his wine, offering

Margun none. "I was wrong. Bravos are mindless thugs: brutal and filthy and unimaginably cruel. They particularly delight in causing pain, usually on the scrats."

"Scrats, sire?"

"Whores of the alleyways with no protectors or owners. Scrats are the lowest of prostitutes. They have no masters, belong to no brothels, and no one cares what happens to them. They're fair game to the bravos, for robbery and for rape."

Margun shrugged.

"You do not care for whores?"

Margun smiled suddenly and Liall saw that his teeth were a bit crooked, with sharp canines. "Whores are fine, in their place. I'm a man after all, so I've paid my share of them."

"Poor treatment of them would not distress you?"

"I merely think that any whore's accusations would be difficult to prove."

"Just so. And?"

The grin persisted. "So perhaps the bravos are not so mindless, after all."

Liall grunted and poured a cup of wine for Margun. "Sit." He slid the cup toward him. "Tell me what punishment you would have handed out for a bravo who *was* somehow prosecuted."

Margun sat and reached carefully for the wine. He looked down into the cup for a moment before drinking. "What is the punishment for rape in Volkovoi?"

"Castration and death by fire, if committed on a noble, whether man or woman."

"What about the common men and women? They at least have some rights, I assume?"

"A few. Noble blood is not as rare in the south as here, but they're even more proud of it. A flogging and a heavy fine would be the punishment for rape of a commoner. Perhaps even death, if the victim were young or a virgin. There are few prisons in the ports, so incarceration would not be an option."

"And for a scrat?"

Liall tapped his cup with his ring-finger. He did not approve of this man yet, but neither did he dislike him. It was clear that Margun was used to thinking and knowing the facts before he answered. "For a scrat, nothing. Of course, nothing."

"This is assuming I would be the man in charge of maintaining the peace in this loathsome port? Very well." Margun drained the rest of his wine in one gulp and placed the cup back on the table. "Then I would find the woman or boy the bravo had raped, and I would bring the man to them. I would let them watch as I cut off the bravo's privates and stuffed them in his mouth." He slid a fingertip down the side of the sweating cup and raised his eyes to meet Liall's.

A changeable nature, Liall thought. *His eyes turn dark when he's angry.*

"Rape is a foul act," Margun said. "Moreover, it is unnecessary, especially for men like us who can find or pay for partners quite easily. For these bravos… their Rshani blood would assure that few could fight them off, and their pay should have been more than enough to buy the poor goods they were taking by force. I would be left with the conclusion that it was their natural inclination to be so foul and there was no chance of repentance."

"I'm certain there would be some repentance at the moment of incision," Liall said, amused despite the grisly conversation.

"Yes, but only for being caught, not for the crime."

Liall tilted his cup to Margun, signaling a victory. "And now to the real question: how do you expect a Hilurin to act?"

Margun's eyebrows drew together and he breathed in deeply. "May I speak plainly?"

"Oh, please do. I've no dearth of courtiers willing to lie to me."

"I am not a courtier, sire."

Liall nodded. "Go on."

"You are the king of Rshan and a Camira-Druz. If you choose to take a Hilurin into your bed, it's not my place to say it's wrong. I won't criticize my king or question his decisions. I was a boy, then I was a soldier, then I was a Setna. Now I'm a soldier again, but without a command. Jarek doesn't want me on her flank and I can't say I blame her, but I'm not ready to go into retirement and I believe I can still be of use to you. If you think I'm the man to guard your consort and keep him safe from your enemies, to wear his badge and to kneel and pledge him—and you—my loyalty, then I will do it. I know nothing of Hilurin. I'm sure I will make mistakes with him, but they will be ones of etiquette, not security."

Margun stood and put his hand on his hip where his sword would have been if Tesk had let him into the room armed. "I will tell you this: If you choose me as master ser Keriss's guard, I will die before seeing him come to the slightest harm. I swear this on my honor."

"You'll swear by more than that." Liall looked up. He could afford no misunderstandings now, no insincere courtly words or polite mouthings about honor. "If he is harmed under your care, or taken by my enemies, I will take more than honor away from you. You have a son in Sul, yes? Some by-blow from a lady who is barely fit to be in noble company. For your boy's sake, I sincerely hope you're fond of him." He took a scroll from his desk and tossed it on the table between them. "Here is a list of your family, your friends, your acquaintances, your lovers past and present… even the name of a courtesan you favor, and your pet hawk. Be assured that none of them are beyond my reach, should you fail me."

He watched how Margun took his threat. The man didn't even blink.

"You may go."

Margun bowed and turned. He hadn't inquired if the appointment was his.

When the door closed after him, Liall sent for Alexyin. His once- tutor bowed at the door, and bowed once more when he came closer. Propriety, that was Alexyin's weakness. He could abide nothing out of place.

"Tesk chose well," Liall said gruffly. "How many

candidates were there in all?"

"Six, sire. Five were men of my choosing. Margun is the only man Tesk put forth."

Liall pulled at a bit of loose skin on the pad of his thumb where a blister had broken. "I've been practicing a great deal lately," he mused aloud. "My swordmaster says I'm improving over the Morturii style I acquired in Kalaslyn, but I despair of ever being as good as I was."

"Nevoi is a true master," Alexyin said in rare praise.

"There were few great swordsmen in Byzantur, nothing to compare with him," Liall agreed. "Or at least, none that I ever met, thank the gods." He sighed. "This man. Margun. How close are you to him?"

"Not in the least. We were on opposite sides of the schism during the Tribeland campaigns. Jarek wanted his head in a basket and his balls adorning the fangs of a snow bear. I advised against it and the matter went before the queen, who banished Margun to the Setna."

"Who tempered him somewhat, one hopes." Liall rubbed his nose and realized he was fidgeting. "How does Tesk know him?"

"They were boyhood friends. He campaigned for Margun's life most fervently with the queen. He said there were precious few men of conscience left in the world, and we could not afford to waste even one."

"I'd have to trust him to be with Scarlet a great deal," Liall hedged. "At least he's not handsome."

Alexyin only smiled and plucked at the hem of his sleeve.

"Oh?" Liall's brows went up.

"I think what the king means is that Margun is not *his* kind of handsome. It's been my observation that you prefer prettier men for yourself. I don't believe the ladies of the court share your view on the matter of ser Margun."

"As long as Scarlet does, I don't particularly care," Liall said crossly. Damn it all, why did Alexyin always make him feel so obvious?

"My lord did not particularly *specify* that the man should be ugly," Alexyin pointed out.

I guess that's his notion of being delicate. Liall saw the wine was nearly empty and wished for another bottle, but did not call for the steward. *That's another thing I'm doing too much of. I can't drown my desire in my cups. The wine here is very good, though, and it makes me yearn for Scarlet less. I have to make more time to see him, more time for the both of us. I'll do it tonight.*

He pushed the scroll of Margun's particulars into the desk. "Cancel the meeting with the emissary of Hnir tonight. No… wait. Delay it. Don't cancel. Not after that speech I made today." He made a face, then turned his back and busied himself sorting scrolls. When he heard the door open, he assumed Alexyin had left.

Alexyin cleared his throat. Liall looked up and saw Scarlet in the doorway. He looked unsure of himself, as he always did when encountering Alexyin.

Liall waved him in. "Come, come. I was hoping you weren't busy."

Scarlet smiled and limped inside, favoring the injured leg a little less than before. He wore a smoke-gray virca trimmed in crimson, with a black velvet collar and a heavy, filigreed silver necklace draped over his shoulders. With his scant height and black hair, he looked like a sketch out of some storybook, delicate and otherworldly, a magical foreign prince out of legend.

Liall hugged him tightly, bending his neck to smell the sweetness of his hair. "You've been using that scented soap again," he murmured close to Scarlet's ear. "I like that."

Alexyin watched the two of them for a moment before leaving silently, which gave Liall a feeling of unease. Alexyin could not move past Cestimir's death. It was as if he believed his life had ended with Cestimir's. Alexyin had lost the focus of his life, not once, but twice now, and Liall worried that he would not be able to find it again. Perhaps Jochi shouldn't be the only Setna to return to the Blackmoat.

Scarlet slipped his hands up Liall's back and hugged him in return. "I was wondering if you were going to avoid me all night."

"You know very well I haven't been avoiding you."

Scarlet kissed Liall's neck and touched his tongue to his skin, and Liall felt a shiver go up his back. *So I like prettier men than Margun, do I? Well, this one is quite the prettiest I've ever seen, but I love him for more than his beauty.*

"Keep that up and I'll have to lock the door," Liall murmured, reaching down to cup one firm buttock in his hand. He squeezed. "Good thing you landed on your leg and not this."

"I'd have had to sleep on my belly for a while."

"How terrible for me."

Scarlet chuckled and nipped his ear. "Are you going to spend the evening with me or not?"

"Biting now, are we?" Liall growled playfully and pretended to devour Scarlet's neck. "But it's your old wolf who has a taste for you tonight. Ooh, and you're so *tender*..."

They tussled and laughed and held each other, until the door opened unannounced. Liall frowned and looked over Scarlet's shoulder. He saw Alexyin had returned with a scroll in his hand. A messenger in the purple baronial tabard of Tebet trailed behind him.

One look at Alexyin's face told Liall that something was wrong. Scarlet looked too, and cursed under his breath. He tried to pull away.

Liall held his arms locked about Scarlet, reluctant to let him go so soon. "No, wait."

"You know bloody well whatever he's come for will take time," Scarlet murmured.

Liall let him go. His arms felt empty.

"I'll be in our rooms," Scarlet said. "Send word when you're coming, please. Or if you're not."

Liall almost called him back, but Alexyin was watching and it was too late. Scarlet was gone, a slender figure retreating down the long hallway. Liall set his jaw and glared at Alexyin.

"What?" he asked flatly.

Alexyin held out the scroll. Liall took it and broke the seal. He scanned the message and his eyes narrowed to slits. He crumpled the scroll in his fist.

"You are his man?" he asked the messenger. The man was older and his boots and purple tabard were spattered with mud; a sign he had ridden in haste and not stopped to freshen before presenting himself at court.

The messenger bowed briefly. "I am Baron Ressanda's messenger, sire. Shall I take your answer to him?"

Alexyin nodded. "I'll fetch the scribe."

"Hold." Liall stepped forward and locked eyes with the messenger. The man bowed his head deeper. "Baron Ressanda wants an answer. Does he think he can bully his king with…" Liall shredded the paper and dropped it at the messenger's feet. "With this feeble threat? There's more strength in watered wine than in this missive."

The messenger looked at his boots. "I'm sure my lord meant no threat whatsoever to his king, sire. I'm certain of it."

"Be certain of this instead," Liall returned coldly. "Be certain I will not be *pressured* to bestow a crown on any House that would deny my kingdom the safety of arms, or of aid when it is called for. Be certain I will remember those who came when the king sounded the horn of war, and those who sat in their castles waiting to see which way the tide turned. Treason is a short rope to hang one's self with, messenger. Tell *that* to your good baron, and tell him I expect the men I commanded of him to report to Khatai Jarek at the fortress of Starhold at once. *All* of them. Not one man less."

"But my lord," the messenger stammered.

"Get out."

The man fled.

"Close the door," Liall said to Alexyin. He strode to the desk and picked up the wine bottle to pour the last of it into his cup. "Send to my consort that I will be some time here. He should sleep."

Alexyin looked uncomfortable. "Perhaps I should have made the messenger wait."

"You did the right thing." Liall sipped the wine but it was tasteless and unsatisfying to him. "Ressanda feels his power at last, does he? He would never have dared challenge my lady mother so. I don't know whether to be alarmed at that or happy that Tebet feels so secure against the north. The eastern baronies seem strong enough to withstand what is happening here."

"Was there a challenge in his missive?"

"Not that you could tell from the subject matter. He's too smart to put that in writing. Ressanda merely stated that the soldiers I commanded of him would be *delayed* in their arrival. He mentioned Ressilka and sent her *noble* regards."

"Meaning that a future queen would be in much more haste to aid her royal betrothed, if such a match were confirmed openly."

Liall raised his cup to toast the east. "Here's to Ressanda. Not exactly a master of tact, is he? He makes it plain that his military support depends upon whether or not I put a crown on his daughter's little red head."

Alexyin cleared his throat. "The noble Lady Ressilka is very lovely as well as skilled in matters of—"

Liall slammed his cup down so hard that he spattered his virca with wine. "I don't care if she can dance with a dinner table on her head. I don't *want* her, Alexyin! Lovely and capable as she is, I don't want her and I don't want to hurt Scarlet. He's compromised so much for me already. I can't ask this of him."

Alexyin frowned and folded his arms. "Pardon me, sire, but what exactly has ser Keriss given up for you? He's exchanged being a poor peasant trader surviving on the edge of the Bledlands for living in a palace as the consort of a king. How is that a step down?"

Liall looked at Alexyin with pity. "You miss the heart of this by a league. You don't understand Hilurin at all, or you would never ask that. I can see why you don't like each other."

"I never said that, my lord."

"You don't like him," Liall snapped. "Do you think Scarlet should feel honored that he's halfway around the world from everything he knows and loves and is familiar with? He's surrounded by strangeness, hostility, danger, and fear here. He stays only for me, Alexyin. Not for the soft silks in his bed or the luxury or for the gold that could be his just for the asking. None of that means much to a true Hilurin, and Scarlet is the truest I've ever known. Family is their deity, as much as that almighty hearth-goddess they pray to day and night. Loyalty is valued over possessions or rank, and a Hilurin man without a family is counted as being worth very little. Scarlet stays in Rshan *for me,* and no other reason." He looked away, his throat tight. "He is the only man I've ever known who loved me solely for myself, who wants nothing of me in return *except* myself. I'm not a king to him. I'm his lover and his love. He has made me his family, and he trusts me utterly. You don't know what that means to me. Or to him."

Alexyin's face was cold, unmoved. "And just how could he leave?"

Liall's eyes narrowed. "What?"

"I said: how could he leave?" Alexyin repeated. "He must stay in Rshan, with you, whether he wishes to or no. He has no choice. What ship would bear him, a *lenilyn* outlander? Who in your entire kingdom would aid him in abandoning his king? No one. So it's rather a poor virtue to say he *stays* for you when he cannot possibly do otherwise."

"I'm not Scarlet's king and he is not my prisoner!" Liall flared.

Alexyin merely looked at him. "You would release him and send him home if he asked it of you?"

Liall closed his mouth. "He wouldn't ask," he said after a moment. "He does not wish to leave me."

"And how do you really know that, if he never has the choice?"

"He's chosen already. He asked me to take him to Rshan. I did. I gave him the choice to leave me before I was made king. He didn't want it. What shall I do, chase after him day and night whining to know if he wishes to leave me? Deva's shrieking hell, he's not an infant!"

"Why are you so angry, sire?"

"Because—" Liall groped for words. He raked his hair back and sighed. "Because I don't deserve his love. I've done… the things I've done with my life have not been worthy of the blood I carry. You don't know, Alexyin. I wasn't a good man in Byzantur. I was a common thief in the Omara hills before I was a Kasiri. When I became an atya, I was still a thief, but I had a krait full of lawless nomads behind me to call it a culture rather than a crime. Anyone who wasn't a Kasiri was fair game, and when someone got in our way and would not be moved, we didn't bargain or send messengers or sign a treaty. We killed him."

"We, or you, my lord?"

"I was in command. It doesn't matter. People died, isn't that enough? I didn't even have the luxury of calling it war. Kasiri are bandits, not soldiers." Liall found his chair and sat heavily. "I chose to be a criminal. I chose to be a brute because it was easier than remembering who I really was and trying to live up to it." *I feel old,* he thought.

"A crime against foreigners would hardly be considered a crime here, sire," Alexyin pointed out.

"Because *lenilyn* are not truly people and have no rights. Yes, I know. I've heard that a thousand times already and so has Scarlet, poor lad. Scarlet knows me in a way that you or my people never will. I treated him terribly when we met, did you know? No, I suppose that story never made it here. I treated him badly, being the man I was then. I frightened him. I attempted to misuse him. I even threatened his life. He knew me at my worst, and he saw through it and fell in love with me anyway. That is a rare gift, Alexyin, for another person to see every ugliness in you and still be able to find that part of you that they can love, that can love them back. Scarlet forced me to see what I had become. At the cost of everything he knew and loved before me, he brought me back to myself. The debt I owe him cannot be repaid by taking a wife and putting her in his rightful place."

Alexyin's cold expression changed. "You fear this marriage more than he does."

Liall shrugged. "I fear losing what is most precious to me. *To me,* Alexyin. You and Jochi and everyone else think I'm stalling merely to spare Scarlet's feelings, but it's much more than that. I lost myself as a Kasiri once, I could easily do the same again as a king. Scarlet expects the best of me, so I try my damnedest not to disappoint him. Is that so wrong?"

It was several moments before Alexyin replied. "I owe your t'aishka an apology, I think."

Liall's interest was piqued. "Why? Did you argue?" Scarlet had said nothing of it, if they had. *But then, he wouldn't.*

Alexyin pulled a chair up and sat. "No, we have not argued," he sighed. "We have not said much of anything to each other."

"Scarlet does not need words to know what a man is thinking. He's deeply intuitive. All his folk are."

Alexyin looked uncomfortable. "That might be why we distrust them so."

"Speak for yourself."

"If he hadn't gone out with Cestimir that day—"

Liall's hand cut the air. "*No.* Don't say it. Vladei's heart was set toward murdering my brother long before Scarlet arrived. If there is blame, it is all mine. My mother warned me about Vladei. I knew he was a threat, but it was my past that stayed my hand." He closed his eyes. "I did not want to be called Kinslayer again. I did not want Vladei's blood on my hands, so I allowed him to live. That's how I'm repaid for mercy." He looked at Alexyin. "Have you said anything to Scarlet about Cestimir?"

"I'm not a fool, my lord."

Liall nodded. "Do not ever. He took Cestimir's death very hard. He blames himself enough for ten of you."

"One day, you must forgive yourself for Nadei, my lord. It has been more than sixty years. He is at peace now."

"Is he? I'm not so sure. I would not rest easy if it were him on my throne, in my place, and my body entombed in ice in the Kingsdal." Liall loosened the collar of his virca and leaned back in his chair. "If Ressanda is serious about withholding his men, we are in deep trouble. Jarek has thirty thousand soldiers at the ready, but I can't bleed off the entire army northward and leave Nau Karmun undefended. Sul will give us five thousand more, but I need another five thousand from Uzna. The barony of Uzna Minor has enough to defend their borders, but none to spare. That leaves me twenty thousand short. The eastern baronies have those men to spare, but they will only send them if Baron Ressanda openly allies with me. They will follow his lead."

"Will Uzna Minor support you?"

"My dear step-brother Eleferi will do whatever his sweet wife tells him to do."

Alexyin's mouth curved. "And how is the Lady Shikhoza?"

"Simmering, although she seems to have recovered from her court banishment." Shikhoza had been given the choice to either wed Eleferi or be exiled to Hnir or S'geth or as far away as Liall could pack her. "After her association with Vladei, I could not have her in the palace. I'd as soon have trusted Vladei to continue living here."

"So the answer is no."

Liall gave Alexyin a wry smile. "Perhaps you do not remember the Lady. Tall, golden-haired, all the sweet sensitivity of a viper? Never mind that it's greatly in the interest of her lands to uphold the crown, if she thinks withdrawing her support would stick a pin in me, she might well do it. If it were a lesser matter, she'd do it just for spite, but the Ava Thule are a deadly serious business. Her lands are in danger as well. She will convince Eleferi to send the soldiers I ask for, but there will be a price."

"Ah," Alexyin said archly. "When is there not? Do you think she wants to return to court?"

"Perhaps. She may have become accustomed to Uzna Minor by now. It's no small city. She can play the supreme lady in a way she never could here." Liall sniffed his disdain and sighed once more. "I think I'll go practice with my swords. Fighting always clears my head."

Alexyin stood. "Shall I come with you?"

"No," Liall said. "But you can tell Scarlet I will be late. Will you do that for me?"

Alexyin bowed. "Of course. Good night, my lord."

Liall hoped Alexyin would make good use of the opportunity to amend his relationship with Scarlet. Both men mourned Cestimir, though Scarlet's heart was not as rent as Alexyin's. Both suffered from guilt over the manner of

Cestimir's murder. Perhaps if Alexyin forgave Scarlet, they could start again.

For Liall's part, there was nothing to forgive.

He stood and took up his cloak, thinking of the little brother he had barely known before Vladei had murdered him. *If anyone is to blame for Cestimir's death, I am.*

He should have acted sooner. He would not make the same mistake again. Ressanda would do well to beware.

The floor was sawdust and sand layered on rough stone. Liall could feel the scrape of it beneath his boots, and the uneven ruts between the paving stones waiting to catch his heels and trip him. Nevoi said that too many sword-fighters wound up dead because they were accustomed to fighting on a level floor.

The room Nevoi had chosen to spar in today was in a long corridor of the stables below the palace armory. The ceiling was low and Liall could hear horses stamping their hooves and restless in their stalls. They were warhorses and the sound of clashing blades never failed to stir their blood.

"Again!"

Liall's breath whistled in his throat as he brought his sword up to guard. Nevoi was not even winded, damn him. The man was also swift and damnably difficult to see in the dim lantern light.

Nevoi lunged, making Liall leap back as the point of

Nevoi's sword stabbed toward his belly. He had begun learning with blunted blades, but that lasted for one day only. When the swordmaster realized that Liall took too many risks during sparring, and was fond of high, slashing arcs that left his body open to attack, he had removed the blunted blades.

"You're lazy," he had told Liall scornfully. "You've gotten soft, fighting little *lenilyn* all those years. You might have gotten away with those flashy techniques when your opponents were a head shorter than you, but you won't do it with me. A good cut or two will remind you that this isn't about pretty dancing with a blade in your hand. It's about survival."

Liall had nursed several small, artfully-placed slashes the first week, then he had learned better.

He turned to follow Nevoi's feint to the right and slashed. Nevoi danced effortlessly out of his reach.

"Stand still, damn you," Liall snarled.

Nevoi laughed. He was younger than Liall by half a century, with merry blue eyes and a wicked grin that Liall swore would fit better on a Minh pirate. He was several inches shorter than Liall, with a slightly round face and snubbed nose below a mane of silvery hair that he kept tied tightly at the nape of his neck. When unbound, Nevoi's thick hair came down to his shoulders and framed his face in jagged bangs. He reminded Liall of a white tiger he'd seen caged in Ankar.

They made another turn at each other, Nevoi stabbing, dodging back, spinning on the ball of his foot like a dancer. Liall panted, holding his own but knowing he'd be no match for Nevoi if they ever fought in earnest. Liall had killed more men in battle than Nevoi had years, but Nevoi was in the full flush of youthful strength and could do this all day.

"Enough!" Liall dropped his stance and took a step back. Nevoi deftly spun and slammed the pommel of his sword into Liall's stomach. Liall coughed and bent over.

"What did I tell you?" The merry glint was gone from Nevoi's eyes.

Liall straightened up, rubbing the ache in his belly. "Never drop my guard until you have dropped yours."

Nevoi nodded. His scowl was forbidding.

"Am I still such a disappointment, ser?"

"You were never a disappointment, my lord," Nevoi said, sliding easily from the role of swordmaster to subject. "Only somewhat vexing."

Liall grinned. "You've been talking to Scarlet again."

"Your t'aishka is an apt pupil and never forgets a lesson. I have not had to mark him as I have you, sire. He has no need of the same correction twice. If he were not so small, he would be a formidable enemy with a blade in his hand, or two of them, as he prefers. Did he ever say who taught him?"

"You haven't asked?" Privately, Liall had always assumed that Nevoi believed his king had taught Scarlet how to use the double Morturii long-knives.

"I know it wasn't you." At Liall's look, Nevoi laughed. "Your pardon, sire, but he never learned those dirty moves from a Rshani warrior. My guess is that it was someone from considerably lower birth with a considerably higher desire for survival, not to mention a hazardous occupation. I've known

Khetian raiders with more scruples than ser Keriss with a long-knife in his hand."

Liall was pleased. "He tasked you, did he? Good."

"Only the first day. I will not discourage him from such low methods, either. He's small and needs every edge he can get. By the Shining Ones, he's *fast,* sire. No swordmaster taught him that. That's all him."

Liall crossed the small sparring space and placed his sword into Nevoi's waiting hand. "It's all Hilurin. Most of the young ones are quick, but he has a true gift, I grant you. The man who taught him was named Rannon, I believe. A Morturii *karwaneer.*"

Nevoi tilted his head in interest.

Liall knew that Nevoi would not ask further without invitation. It would be impolite to question a king so. "A master of trade caravans. In the south they trade between Morturii and Byzantur, and the lands between Minh and beyond," he supplied. "It's a dangerous life. Scarlet rode with them for half a year."

Nevoi's eyebrows went up. "How old was he?"

"Fifteen or so."

"So young as that?" Nevoi picked up an oil-cloth.

"You disapprove?"

"Not precisely, sire." Nevoi oiled the blades swiftly and replaced them in their leather sheaths. "I know something of Byzantur custom. I'm surprised he was allowed to take to the road at such an age."

"He had the wilding."

"Ah!" Nevoi smiled. "That explains it. I knew he was different. He loves the mechanics of sword fighting rather than the pure art of it, but for different reasons than most men. For him, it is a skill like making fire or mending your boots: something one needs to sustain life."

"If only you knew how well he could make fire," Liall said cryptically. Again, Nevoi turned that arch look on him. "You'd heard my ship was attacked at sea during the crossing? Scarlet set the sails of the Minh ship afire from the deck of our brigantine. I had not looked for him during the frenzy and blood of the battle, but suddenly he was there and then the sails were on fire. He has never confessed it, but later… I put it together."

"I have heard of Hilurin magic," Nevoi said thoughtfully, "but I did not know it was so strong. Interesting."

"How so?"

"To attack across a distance longer than a man's reach of sword or spear is forbidden in Byzantur and Morturii. To carry a bow is a death sentence for most men. But if a man used magic…"

Liall nodded slowly. It made perfect sense. "I marvel that I haven't realized it before. Those laws are old, perhaps back to the time when the Hilurin first journeyed south and landed on the shores of Byzantur. I can see where a law meant to forbid the use of magic could be translated into a law forbidding ranged weapons, after that magic has been hidden and forgotten for centuries. Scarlet was shocked when it happened, and frightened. I don't think he even *meant* to do it."

"Such a skill would make ser Keriss a powerful adversary

indeed. It's a talent that could save his life, if he honed it well."

"You think he should try?"

"I think he is strong, but even if he were the strongest Hilurin in all the world, a Rshani opponent could snap his neck like a kitten. *If* the man could ever lay hands on him."

"If," Liall agreed. Again, Nevoi made sense. The swordmaster was a valuable man, indeed.

"I will consider it," Liall promised, "but for now, I must take my leave of you." He bowed shortly to Nevoi, student to master. "I thank you for the instruction."

Nevoi bowed back, much lower than Liall. He only allowed Liall to forget who was king when they were on the practice floor. "My lord honors me."

They parted and Liall wished he could go immediately to Scarlet, to see the smile on his face and touch the softness of his skin. The intense attraction he had felt for Scarlet in the beginning had never faded, not even a little. Now, more than ever, he yearned to be with him, but one more matter required his attention.

He found the fire dying down in his solar. The guard lit some candles for him, threw four logs on the hearth, and left with a bow. Liall poured pale green wine into a cup. He sat and drank slowly, thinking over what he must say. When he'd finished two cups, he took a deep breath and found a sheet of vellum.

It was not every day that he summoned an Ancient to the Nauhinir.

Fire and Burning

Dvi, the cook, waited by the table and held a chair for him. Scarlet frowned. No matter how often he told Nenos that such things were unnecessary, the polite old steward would smile and nod and then go about doing things the way he had always done them.

When he complained to Liall about how awkward it made him feel to have a chair held for him—a thing only done for women and the elderly in Scarlet's experience—Liall had shrugged.

"Nenos runs my household in the manner he thinks best," he had said. "On some matters, he won't be moved. Unlike your homeland, there are no slaves here. Men and women serve by choice, and capable servants are most valued. They can also make life very difficult if they wish to. It would not be easy to convince him that his methods are incorrect."

So Scarlet sighed and took the chair Dvi held for him. The dining hall was less formal than the one in their old chambers, thank the gods. Still, it was luxurious by his standards, and huge. The meal laid out on the trestle table was a variety of spiced dumplings stuffed with ginger pork or fruit jam. It was a dish he often requested, but one that Liall did not care for. Word that the king would not be dining with him must have reached the servants.

Dvi served the che in silence. A guard entered the room

and signaled to Dvi, who bowed and left to speak with him. He returned in moments.

"You have a visitor, ser," he told Scarlet.

Scarlet sipped the che and wondered if he should send for wine instead. At least he'd be able to sleep. "Who?"

"I hope you will forgive this intrusion." Alexyin appeared in the doorway, his hands clasped and his spine stiff.

"I already know the king isn't coming," Scarlet sighed. "He didn't have to send you." His leg ached and he made a conscious effort not to rub it. His arm had healed quickly, but it had only been bruises and scrapes there. The gash on his leg was deep and it had hurt more than he let Liall know.

Alexyin glanced at the sparse meal on the table. "The king sends his apologies. He is delayed."

His voice was neutral, as always. Scarlet waved his hand at the dishes. "Are you hungry? It's a shame to waste it." He turned over a cup and poured green che into the porcelain. The steam had the scent of roses. "Liall likes this kind. A southern blend, he calls it. We had some when we were with the Kasiri. It's still my favorite." He pushed the cup forward and looked at Alexyin expectantly.

Alexyin sat down like he was lowering himself into a mud puddle. He put one finger on the cup but did not drink. "Thank you, ser."

Scarlet held back a sigh. *I've heard warmer thanks from farmers I gouged for the price of a whetstone.*

"Cheers." He toasted Alexyin and sipped.

Alexyin inclined his head in response but still did not drink.

"You don't like me much, do you?"

That was too blunt for Alexyin. "If I've given offense, I hope the king's t'aishka will forgive me," he said formally.

"Oh, stop it," Scarlet said in disgust. "You don't like me. You never have. I didn't know why at first, and now it doesn't matter. I don't care if you like me or not. I *do* care that you think I don't grieve for Cestimir." Scarlet put a hand on his chest and spoke earnestly. He might not get another chance to talk to Alexyin like this, man-to-man. "Please believe me, Alexyin. I tried to get away, to run for help, but Melev was there and he prevented me. I…" He gestured helplessly. "I wasn't strong enough to save Cestimir. By all the gods, I swear to you that I wanted to."

"But you were strong enough to destroy Melev, whom not even our greatest swordsman could have bested," Alexyin said harshly. "Tell me; how is it that your magic destroyed a creature that not ten of our warriors could bring down, but you could not save the future king of Rshan? Or was it because you wanted Nazheradei to be king?"

Scarlet recoiled. He suddenly realized that Alexyin believed him to be just as sly and evil as Vladei, that he suspected him of helping Liall to the throne over Cestimir's dead body. The thought made him cold, and he recalled it was one of Liall's oldest and most trusted friends that he was alone with. *A true friend will risk much to protect those they are loyal to, even murder.*

I'm beginning to think like one of them.

Scarlet stared at Alexyin, wondering how to reach him. "I am not Rshani," he said quietly. "I'm not one of you. I will never *be* one of you."

Alexyin's glare wavered. "I don't take your meaning." He half-rose from his chair. "I should go, ser." He looked at Dvi, who shot an uncertain look at Scarlet.

"Sit down," Scarlet commanded. When he obeyed, Scarlet took a deep breath and leaned forward.

"You keep expecting me to act like one of you, like a Rshani would, and you don't know me. You don't know my kind at all." He held up his left hand with the missing finger, turning it so Alexyin could see the difference clearly.

"Isn't this enough to prove I'm not like you? That I'm not like Vladei or Shikhoza or whoever you imagine? Your politics, these ambitions… I don't have them. I don't care about power or wealth or having men obey my commands. I'm only here because I wouldn't leave Liall, and now *he* can't leave. I would have preferred Cestimir to be king. Liall and I would probably be on our way back home by now, and happier to boot. We'd damn sure have more time together." He gritted his teeth. "I don't like your buggering land. It's too cold. There's no sun. I don't recognize the trees or plants or the songs the birds make, and there's no one here with a face like mine. You speak my language but none of you know anything about Hilurin beyond legends of evil magic, and everyone here mistrusts me, is frightened of me, or just plain hates me. Cestimir told me you were a wise man, but you wouldn't know a Hilurin heart from a turnip." Scarlet put his hand down, his throat tight. Would he never be done with this suspicion and dislike from Liall's people? "And now you can go."

Alexyin rose slowly, looking down at Scarlet, his hard face as closed and inscrutable as ever. "You have spoken plainly, so now must I: The king must marry and produce an heir. Only then will his reign be established, the kingdom secure, and his person safe. If you love him so much, put your own feelings aside and convince him of that. Then I may believe that you remain with my king for more than your own benefit."

He was not hurt by the words, but he'd thought better of Alexyin than this. "I've been named *whore* by your lot already, Alexyin. More than once. I'm fucking tired of it."

Alexyin bowed. "I apologize," he said, sounding anything but apologetic.

Dvi showed the man out and did not return, and Scarlet was glad for it. He stared at the cup of che Alexyin had refused to drink. After a while, he picked it up and dashed the liquid into the fire. Coals popped and steam hissed up in a long finger of white, vanishing up the chimney.

Liall is the one thing I truly love about Rshan, and they'd be happy to take him away from me. They might even succeed. What would be left for me here, then?

There were several hours of the evening left and he had little to occupy him. He went to his couch under the big window and tried to read, but the pictures in the Sinha books—sketches of Ancients, snow bears, and patterns of stars—did not please him and the lines of script blurred together. Learning to read made his head ache and the silence of the apartment seemed to ring in his ears. Scarlet turned the page and idly traced his finger over the Sinha script. He recognized several words: *bear, red, sword, battle, love, blood.* Those were words that went well with stories. Raja meant red, and in a way so did Keriss.

"Red," he murmured, his index finger following the curling lines of the word.

It began to glow.

He was so shocked that he threw the book to the floor. He pulled his feet up into the chair and looked down. The book had fallen page-down, its spine facing the ceiling.

Did I imagine that?

He stared at the book for long minutes, almost afraid that it would come alive and go flapping around the room like some demon-bird. Slowly, his courage returned and he reached to pick it up. The pages sighed together normally. When he rested it in his lap and turned the leaves, nothing happened. Nothing happened when he traced the letters again, and even when he found the initial word for *red* and attempted to repeat his actions exactly, nothing happened.

I'm idle too often. Mum always said idleness made me moody and prone to silly fancies. Maybe I did imagine it.

But he knew he had not. This ability was something new with his Gift, and unlike the incident with the apple tree, he had no clue what it could be used for. What good were glowing words on a page? It wasn't like a healing chant or lighting a damp fire. It seemed very wrong that he should even be *able* to do something so useless with his magic. Everyone knew that Deva's Gift was meant to help the Hilurin survive in a harsh world. Glowing words couldn't do that.

He shook his head and got up to replace the book in the heavy wooden case. "Silly books," he muttered. "Maybe Mum was right." He abandoned trying to puzzle it out and began to undress for bed.

When Liall returned late in the night, he pretended to be asleep.

"Up! Keep your guard up, I say!"

Golden motes of hay drifted through the torch light as Scarlet circled his opponent with a sparring long-knife in each hand. No matter how much Nevoi spat and shouted, Scarlet persisted in going for the low point, dodging under every one of Nevoi's slashes and darting past him, behind him, always appearing where he was least expected. The horses stamped and snorted in their stalls, their instincts enticed by the sounds of combat. Nevoi's sword clanged against Scarlet's blunted blade, shearing sparks as Scarlet slipped past the attack once more. Another feint from Nevoi, pressing him on the left. He dropped his guard and dodged right, keeping Nevoi at bay with the dangerous point of his blade. Nevoi cursed and tried to bat his long-knife aside. Clashing steel rang like a bell.

"Guard up!" Nevoi roared.

He was running out of breath. Scarlet spun on the ball of one foot, favoring his injured leg, turning, his long-knife slashing the air in a wide arc…

And hit nothing. Nevoi was no longer there. A cold line

of metal kissed the side of Scarlet's throat.

"Circles close, little one," Nevoi panted close to his ear as they both stood frozen in fighting stance. "There's your weakness."

"I yield," Scarlet wheezed, drawing in ragged breaths of air.

"I accept," Nevoi grunted. The blade of the swordmaster rang as he slammed it back into the hilt at his waist. "Explain yourself."

Scarlet dropped his stance and lowered the double long-knives. His arms felt heavy as stone. "How do you mean?"

"I told you to keep your guard up."

Scarlet shook his head. His leg ached fiercely and it stung where the stitches had pulled against his skin. Esiuk was supposed to cut them out later today. "Keeping my guard up won't do much good if the man can smash me like an acorn. You're too strong. I can't just guard and take the hit. I'd get hammered."

"So you disobeyed my instructions, ignored my lesson?"

Scarlet straightened his back and shrugged.

Nevoi smiled. "Good." He slapped Scarlet's arm. "Very good. Next time, you practice with the sperret."

"Oh, no you don't." Scarlet limped with him to the alcove where their edged weapons hung on an old quintain packed in from the sparring yard. "I'm not letting you that close." A sperret was a short, stabbing foil, more like a thick needle than a knife. It was a light weapon that could be easily hidden and quickly deployed. Kasiri fighters were known to favor the sperret, and so were women.

"Tradition says the sperret must be practiced with a shield. It's a good weapon for small fighters, even better than the long-knife."

"It's a weapon for a girl or a thief."

"We will not argue the point," Nevoi conceded with good grace. "But I insist that you try, at the least. If it's not your weapon, we will soon know it. You may be wiser than I when it comes to your limits."

Nevoi always pushed him to the brink of what he was capable of, and the master steadfastly refused to allow Liall to witness their sparring.

"The young man is not your consort when he's under my training," he had informed the king, "but my student, and only that. If you wish for me to instruct him, you will allow me to do it in my customary way or you must find another teacher."

Liall had been put out, but even he listened to Nevoi on matters of the sword.

"I wasn't aware I had any limits," Scarlet said with a cockiness he did not feel.

"Good. Never let me convince you otherwise."

Scarlet's sword belt hung from the battered, ancient helmet of the quintain. Nevoi took it down and briefly admired the twin pair of curved Morturii long-knives. The steel was pure black etched with silver in wondrous shapes depicting the violent Hilurin tale of Deva's creation of the world.

"I never tire of seeing these weapons," he said. He traced his finger over the spun wire of the hafts, which had no guards. "They're quite beautiful. How did you come by them?"

Scarlet smiled, remembering Masdren's leather shop and his pack of noisy little children. "In Ankar. They were a gift from a friend of my father's."

"Is all the metalwork in Ankar so fine?"

"Yes. And my knives were not even made by a true master. Just an ordinary smith in the souk. The Morturii are wondrous fond of iron. Suits them, I guess. The soldiers are just about as hard, and they forge better steel than the Minh, even."

"I have never met a Minh," Nevoi said thoughtfully. He handed Scarlet the sword belt.

"Trust me, you don't want to." Scarlet buckled the belt around his waist.

"Was this Masdren a smith?"

"A leatherworker. He made the sheaths, see?" Scarlet turned to show Nevoi the craftsmanship of the tooled leather, black to match the knives.

"Black steel is rare in Rshan," Nevoi said. "Our land lacks the minerals to forge it properly, and the Morturii charge a dear price to trade for them. Since a bright sword cleaves as well as a dark one, it doesn't seem worth the cost. That is, until you see black steel for yourself. Then nearly anything is worth it."

Several of the horses lifted their heads and neighed. From the far end of the stables, a huge set of iron-barred doors creaked mightily as they parted, letting in a rush of chilly air. Shadows moved over the timbered walls as pale spring daylight crept in. Scarlet could not recall those doors ever being opened when he was present.

The stallion in the nearest stall whickered and twitched his ears, the whites of his eyes showing.

"New additions to the stables," Nevoi said. The sound of shod hooves clacking on stone rang out, and all the stabled horses stirred with interest. "Many, from the sound of them. Shall we go and see?"

Scarlet nodded eagerly. He was infatuated with the fine warhorses of the palace stables, and had made a point of learning all their names. Horses were one of the familiar things of Rshan, though they were much larger than Byzan horses and bred to endure the fierce cold.

A host of men in unfamiliar livery led a double line of horses into the stables. Most were the dappled grays and sables that were the norm for northern breeds, but a matched team of superb white stallions with eyes like red jewels captivated Scarlet.

The white horses were led by a lean, sharp-faced man. He wore purple riding clothes with the badge of a sail on his tunic, and sported the fussiest beard Scarlet had ever seen.

Nevoi frowned. "Tebet colors," he murmured aside to Scarlet. "Perhaps we should go."

Scarlet stared at the proud animals, unwilling to leave. None of the strange grooms or the Nauhinir guards made to speak to him, but he saw Theor, Liall's great bear of a horsemaster, overseeing the process. Scarlet waved to him.

Theor looked alarmed. He shook his head and shot a glowering look at Nevoi.

"Let us leave," Nevoi said, taking Scarlet's arm.

"Ser Keriss!"

Nevoi muttered a low curse and turned with Scarlet. The lean man in purple swaggered in their direction and threw back his cloak so that his sail badge was clearly visible. His clipped beard was a thin line tracing his jaws and meeting in a sharp point on his chin. Scarlet noted his hair and beard had a tinge of red.

"I've wanted to meet you for a long time, ser," the man said in Sinha, stopping a few feet away and hooking his thumbs in his belt. He looked Scarlet up and down and bowed briefly. "Lord Jarad Hallin, of Tebet."

It took Scarlet a moment to translate the words the man had spoken. "You know me, ser?" he replied in Sinha. He knew his accent was poor, though he practiced it daily.

Hallin turned his head and spoke in rapid-fire Sinha to the grooms and armed men accompanying him. Scarlet could not follow it, but the men in purple laughed and cast scornful looks his way.

Scarlet was determined to keep his manners in check. "Pardon me?"

"Don't bother, ser Keriss," Nevoi said in Bizye. "The man is baiting you. Come."

"Baiting?" Hallin said with a grin, his Bizye perfect. "Not at all. I would not so insult the consort of the king. Not when I come bearing the bride-gifts of Tebet."

Scarlet felt his face go hot. "Bride?" he blurted.

"Aye, as I said." Hallin swept a hand expansively toward the horses. "These magnificent animals are a bride-gift from the king's future wife, the Rose Lady of Tebet."

Scarlet's cheeks burned as if he'd been slapped, and he was suddenly very aware that he was armed. Twice armed, if he counted his sparring blades. They were blunted, true, but they would make a nice dent in Hallin's nose.

"I know it's spring, but she's a bit early to the dance, this rose," he said, his back stiff with anger. *Bride? Not if I have anything to say about it. But do I?* "She might find the ballroom empty when she gets there. The king hasn't agreed to marry anyone."

"Formalities." Hallin smirked, placing a hand over his middle and bowing again. "Mere formalities. We expect the announcement daily in Tebet. Everyone knows that the king's dear kinswoman is the logical choice for his queen. Logical, and," he held up a finger, "quite necessary. A monarch must breed and a dynasty must have an heir. Unless…" he touched that finger to his mouth and evinced an air of shock, "unless *you* plan to fill that role for the king?"

Behind Hallin, Theor smacked one of the white stallions on the rump to get him moving. "Let's move it along!" he bellowed. "Are we stabling these beasts or gabbing them to sleep?" His face suffused with an angry color that turned his dark skin the hue of red oak.

Nevoi took the cue and nodded to Hallin. "Good day to you, ser." He took Scarlet's arm in an iron grip and marched him away.

Once they were through the stables and at the foot of the stairs leading into the palace wardroom, Scarlet wrenched his arm from Nevoi, his face burning in shame.

"Why did you do that?"

"To save you from having to speak to a fool."

"I can *speak* for myself," Scarlet said hotly. "I had a thing or two more to say to that puffed-up purple rooster."

"No, you didn't," Nevoi said calmly. "You had much to say to Lady Ressilka, but she wasn't there. Her father's fool was. *Lord* Hallin, my arse!" he snorted. "His lands in Tebet are rotten ice and petrified forests, and he's a mongrel half-blood to boot. He is Ressanda's low creature, one the baron doesn't mind making into a jackass. A true lord would have had more respect for his baron's name than to engage in the farce we just witnessed."

"He was lying, then?"

Nevoi looked down at Scarlet. "What are you afraid of? That your lover will marry without saying a word to you about it and promptly forget you ever existed? That's not the Nazheradei I've come to know."

"I'm not afraid," Scarlet lied.

Nevoi slapped him on the back of his head.

"Ow!" Scarlet rubbed his scalp. "What in three hells was that for?"

"For lying."

"I thought the fucking lessons were over for today," Scarlet muttered dangerously. "And I didn't lie. It's not fear, it's…" He groped for words. "All right, maybe it is fear."

"So fight back. Fear isn't a very useful emotion for a warrior. Rage is better."

"I'm not a warrior. I can't fight back. Not like she does. I don't care for the idea of putting myself in her dress."

Nevoi tilted his head, as if he were trying to puzzle out a particularly good riddle. "Her dress. You mean you don't want to fight like a woman would."

"I can't very well challenge her to swords, now can I?"

"You could. It's been known to happen."

"Liall would have a fit. Besides I'm not fighting any girl."

"That girl is nearly half again your size."

"I don't care!" Scarlet burst out. "She's still a *girl*."

Nevoi chuckled shortly. "There is a place for youthful chivalry in the world, but you'd be a fool to be gracious in this battle. The Rose Lady would smile gently and hike her skirts up so she could plant her heels into your back on her way to the throne. This is not Byzantur, ser. The men of Rshan hold the reins of power in both family and state, but our women are not the soft and obedient creatures of Kalaslyn. Here, they can kill as efficiently as the men, and it is folly to give quarter to an affirmed enemy once the battle is engaged."

Scarlet kicked at an errant bit of hay on the flagstones. "I don't want her as an enemy. I don't want any enemies. I just want to be with Liall for as long as I can. I want some measure of peace and happiness for us. We've damn well earned it."

"Ah, child," Nevoi said sadly. He slid his arm around

Scarlet's shoulders in a comforting gesture. "Did no one ever tell you? There is no peace for kings."

It was very late when Liall returned for sleep. He crept around their bed chamber, obviously trying to be silent as he undressed and pulled off his boots, but Scarlet was wide awake. Someone would have told Liall about the stable and the horses, of course, and about Jarad Hallin and what he had said.

Scarlet could have spoken out and told Liall there was no need for quiet, that he couldn't sleep, but then Liall would have come and tried to soothe him, tried to speak to him, and he wanted that least of all.

The bed dipped as Liall's weight settled in beside him. Scarlet lay there with his back turned to his lover, his will focused on remaining perfectly still. The fire had died down and it was warm enough that no one had come to stoke it again. The smoldering embers were the only light in the room, giving the walls a sullen glow.

"I know you're awake," Liall said quietly into the gloom. "I can tell by your breathing."

Scarlet did not move. "Is it true?" he whispered into his pillow.

Liall hesitated, and Scarlet's heart leapt.

"No," Liall said at last. "I've given them no answer, but neither have I refused."

"Are you sending those horses back?" Scarlet murmured, as if telling a secret. He was afraid if he let his voice rise above a whisper that he might start shouting, and then he might just get up and start breaking things. His anger was like a leashed wolf inside him, but he couldn't turn it on Liall. It wasn't Liall's fault.

"I cannot," Liall said haltingly. "It would be a grave insult to the baron, and I've just asked him for something rather important."

"Important to you?"

"To the realm. If I offend him, he may refuse. That would be disastrous, for I would have to respond to his refusal with steel and blood. A new king with a precarious crown can't afford to look weak. I also can't afford to alienate Tebet. Please try to understand. I would never—"

"Hurt me," Scarlet finished for him. "So you've said. Good night, Liall."

"Scarlet…"

"Good night."

Liall rolled heavily onto his back and sighed deeply. "May I please ask you one thing, at least? I've spoken to Tesk… what happened at the hunt? Tesk said you didn't move when the cat leapt. You're so fast, Scarlet. I've *seen* how fast you can be. Why didn't you move?"

Scarlet had wondered about that himself. "I don't know," he answered. Liall was tensely quiet, and Scarlet thought he understood the root of his lover's fear. "*No*, I didn't deliberately not move. I don't have a death wish, and I won't throw myself off a cliff if you marry Ressilka." He punched his pillow. "I may throw her off one, though."

Liall touched his shoulder gently. "We should talk."

Scarlet pressed his cheek hard to his pillow. "I don't want to talk to the bloody King of Rshan right now. I'm tired. Good night."

Liall did not argue, but he kept his hand on Scarlet's shoulder until he fell asleep. When Scarlet woke up the next morning, Liall had left and his side of the bed was cold.

"No," Scarlet said stubbornly, his arms crossed. He sat in the room he would forever think of as the queen's solarium, no matter that there was no queen now, just a king.

And how long will that last, he thought sourly.

Two weeks had passed since Ressilka's gift of horseflesh had arrived, a span in which he barely saw Liall and in which it had become painfully obvious to Scarlet that the matter of Ressilka was not simply going to go away. Her gifts were in the stables. Her servants were in the palace kitchens. Her emissaries and messengers were constantly present in the inner tier, waiting to pounce on Liall for an audience. Jarad Hallin seemed to be lurking in every hall that Scarlet visited, always with that scornful, knowing smirk stamped in the middle of his beard. Scarlet had even begun to fancy that his own servants—Nenos, Chos, and Dvi—were looking at him with skeptical eyes. *You are not enough,* those eyes seemed to say. *You cannot give the king what he needs most. Only a woman can do that, and there is one waiting.*

Everywhere Scarlet turned, there she was. The very walls seemed to whisper of her, and of endings. He felt harried by that presence, and his temper had grown frayed.

Liall had brought him to the solarium when they first came to Rshan, because he was unaccustomed to the cold, dark months and had begun to sicken from lack of light, suffering from headaches, dizziness, and sudden flares of temper.

I feel sick now. I'm sun-sick. With the light comes a new queen. I could almost wish for winter again, if it meant we could go back to the way things were. I have to tell him. I have to remind him. Like me, he forgot, but we can't live inside a dream.

"I've sat here enough," Scarlet said. He tried to rise and Liall pushed him back down.

"No, you have not," Liall said. "You're snapping at everyone, even Nenos. You need some light."

"I *need* some peace!" Scarlet flung his hand toward the door. "And the sun has returned, you know. I don't need to come in here anymore."

"You do if you refuse to go outside."

Scarlet wanted to. He wanted to hunt and ride, but to do that he needed his horse. Jarad Hallin or one of the Tebet people were always in the stables, pampering Ressilka's white horses, never passing up an opportunity to make some remark that set Scarlet's blood to boiling. He had taken to holing up in his rooms, drinking wine, looking at books he could not read, and staring into the fire as if it held answers.

"I'm happy where I am," he muttered.

"Like hell you are. You're sulking."

"And you're an ass. Now go away and do whatever kings do. Stop vexin' me."

Liall sighed deeply. "You're avoiding me and it can't go on. I've never known you to run from a fight, my t'aishka. You're not a coward to hide from pain. You never were and never will be." He was calm, his voice rational, the same infuriating tone he'd been using for days. "I think I must do this thing," he said regretfully. "Or at least agree to do it at some point."

Scarlet was beginning to think there was no end to the kinds of suffering they had in Rshan. "No," he repeated unhappily.

The solarium was tiled in pale green glass, with a curved ceiling where false light filtered in brightly as moving patterns across the floor and walls. Beyond the first wall of glass, a second wall of mirrors amplified the illumination from the ceiling reflector, giving the greenish light the appearance of sun-dappled leaves. The only decorations were the elaborate wicker chair where Scarlet sat and several potted plants scattered about the floor.

Liall went down on one knee beside the throne-like chair. He would not have knelt if there were anyone else to witness, not even as a joke. A king knelt to no one.

"My sweet love," he murmured, taking Scarlet's hand in his own.

Scarlet sighed. "That's not going to work."

"I'm not trying to wheedle you into anything," Liall said. Then, at Scarlet's look: "Very well. I am. But, Scarlet… love…"

"I can't do it and I want you to stop asking," Scarlet interrupted. His hand tightened around Liall's larger one. "I know what they want of you, and I know you have to give them an answer, but you've answered them before and they're never satisfied with it. They press you and you turn around and press me. Well, I'm fucking tired of being pushed, Liall! If I could do this for you, I would, but I can't." His words fell one upon the other like a rockslide, and he could not stop them. "We've been over this a dozen times. What must I say and how must I say it before it sinks in? Do you want me to write you a letter?"

"I cannot vouch for the translation if you do." Liall smiled faintly.

Jochi had been teaching Scarlet to read and even to pen a little bit in Sinha, though it was a child's scrawl still and it would be several years yet before he learned the Rshani language.

"I'm not in the mood for jokes," he muttered.

"Scarlet, if there were another way—any other way—you know I would take it."

"Making a child is not like building one of your magic engines," Scarlet retorted. "There's more than one road to get to Rusa, as they say. I've given you a map to several. If you need an heir that badly, I'm sure she'd be willing to mother it, but mother is not wife."

"I do not fathom how you can care nothing if I fuck the woman—"

"Oh, I care," Scarlet broke in. "I care a lot, but I'm not stupid. A kingdom *does* need an heir and children don't grow on apple trees. Do what you must and then set her aside."

Liall shook his head. "I knew it was more than just simple jealousy. You were never that petty. But, love, I can't just bed her and claim the child is my heir. I have to *marry* her for that. You don't understand how their minds work."

"You mean Rshani minds."

Liall hesitated, then nodded.

Scarlet pushed him away and rose, heading for the door.

"Scarlet, wait!"

Liall caught him and grabbed his arm gently. Liall, so much larger than he, was always so careful not to hurt him.

Except now. Except like this.

"Please wait," Liall begged. "We can't keep dancing around this matter and sniping at each other. It's making us both miserable. There must be a solution."

"There is," Scarlet said lowly, his face averted. "Send me home." *I have to tell him.*

"You are home." Liall's hand slid under Scarlet's jaw, tenderly tipping his head back to brush his black hair out of his eyes. "You're with me, where you belong. I will never send you away, or allow you to be parted from me. I could not bear it. You know this." Ice-blue eyes stared down at Scarlet, adoring as always, compelling as always. "You *know* it, redbird."

Scarlet twisted to get away, but Liall pulled him close and held him. He relented and pressed his face against the material of Liall's shirt, smelling Rshani spices and musky cologne. His arms went around Liall's broad back and gripped tight.

"If I could do this..." he whispered, his voice muffled.

"We may have no choice, t'aishka," Liall said, brushing his mouth against Scarlet's hair. "A king is less free than anyone."

Scarlet's breath caught. Those were Cestimir's words. Vladei had murdered Cestimir, dragged him into a temple ruin and beheaded him, all because Cestimir was the prince and another wanted his throne. Liall was only king because Cestimir was dead.

"They can't force you," Scarlet murmured.

"Not literally, no. That would be a sight, wouldn't it? But they can do other things—many other things—that would make my life and yours immensely more complicated and unpleasant. We might wind up wishing that we had taken the easier road. If I married her, at least I would have some measure of control. I would still be king, after all, and master of my own house. Any wife of mine must obey me as her husband *and* as her king. I would not allow you to be pushed aside."

"So you say now."

"I will swear by anything you like."

"I don't want promises." Scarlet pulled away slowly and rubbed his face. He felt himself giving in. But Deva, it was hard; it was so hard to agree! He wasn't ready to do that yet, not by far.

He was seized again with an urge to flee, to run and run until he there was no more road to travel on, anything to get away from the truth that gnawed at him, devouring him by inches. In desperation, his gaze went to the water clock stationed by a green-fronded palm, a tall and complicated affair of hollow brass cylinders filled with water that dripped at a steady, predictable rate. A small silver bird was mounted on a plunger atop the largest of the cylinders. The bird's beak pointed to marks on a sliding scale as the water emptied.

"Is that the right hour?"

Liall glanced at the water clock. "Yes. Please listen. Can we at least—"

"I'm late." Scarlet ducked past Liall's arm for the door.

"Scarlet, we haven't finished!"

"I'm late!" Scarlet called back, hurrying in case Liall came after him again. "Jochi expected me an hour ago. I'll see you at dinner!" He rushed out of the solarium and up the steps into the pale stone heart of the great palace, his chest pounding.

One more day. I've put it off another day, but it's not enough. I need years yet and he's not going to give them to me. They won't let him…

There were so many doors in this part of the palace, so many salons and courts and bedrooms and unused halls with no apparent function. Scarlet ducked into the alcove and hid in the deep shadows, waiting for Liall's heavy step to pass him by.

When the sound of boots had faded, he slumped down and hid his face in his hands.

I have to tell him, but not today. Please, gods, not today. Not yet. I just need a little more time.

Scarlet loved the library, loved its soaring, vaulted ceiling and the bookcases that were taller than two men. He loved the padded wooden chairs that were big enough to sleep in, with armrests carved in the shape of wolves, and he loved the rich scents of leather and spices and colognes lingering in the air from a thousand Rshani visitors. It reminded him of Masdren's leather shop, the way it smelled in the middle of the Ankar night, with the aromas of the busy souk drifting past. The library was one of the few places in the Nauhinir he found peaceful.

It was empty except for Jochi, who was waiting for him.

Scarlet's boot-heels hit the wooden floor like drums and echoed against thick walls that were lined floor-to-ceiling with shelves and shelves of books. The book spines were mostly leather, but some were parchment, wood, linen, even shell and precious stones. There were so many colors that it seemed as if the walls were papered with butterfly wings.

Liall's silver and blue banner dominated half of one wall. Other banners of Rshani noble houses were hung about the hall, and Scarlet could recognize several. There was the green, blue and gold banner of Jadizek with its pattern of grain, and there was the black banner of Uzna with its red sickle moon and white star, and closest to Liall's banner was the white standard of Sul with its compass rose below a gold sun.

So many houses, so much history. He felt quite small beneath them. Funny, he had never felt small in Byzantur, even though nearly everyone outside of Lysia had been bigger than him.

Jochi smiled as he rose from his chair and bowed. His hair was unbound, a fall of ice hanging to his waist.

"I'm sorry," Scarlet said at once. "I was with Liall and I didn't realize it was so late, and then—"

Jochi held up his hand to stop him. "Ser Keriss, please. The king does not apologize if he keeps me waiting. His time is more valuable than mine. The king's t'aishka does not need to apologize for keeping one of the king's retainers waiting, either." His voice was mild. "Save the king, there is no one in the Nauhinir with a rank higher than yours. Why must I keep reminding you of this fact?"

Scarlet looked away uncomfortably and found a seat. "You don't. I understand. I don't have to like it, though, all this natter about rank and such. We didn't have to bother with that so much when Liall was just a prince."

Jochi wore a brown virca trimmed in gold, but the sleeves were very short. Scarlet supposed that was a summer fashion. Unlike the common rooms and great halls in the warming days of spring, the library hearth was filled with a roaring fire. He guessed it was to preserve the books, for it had begun to feel damp in some places of the palace. Most of the rooms were heated with wood fires or by strange metal tanks that Liall said were furnaces. They burned a kind of black oil and were hotter than fireplaces. It kept the castle comfortable enough for him, if he dressed warmly.

Jochi chose a book from a case of yellow oak and began to page through it. "King Nazheradei was never 'just' anything. He has always been a most impressive man. And you complained then, too."

Scarlet felt like being a little mean. He leaned back in the deep chair and propped his elbow on the armrest. "He isn't here to hear you, you know."

Jochi's eyebrows went up. "Aye, ser, I know. Does something trouble you?"

Scarlet's eyebrows drew together. "No more than something every day for the last fortnight."

"Ah." Jochi shut the book with a snap and took a seat opposite him. "You mean since Tebet sent their betrothal gift."

"Tebet, or Ressilka?"

"Unless I ask the Lady herself, I can't know. Likely, it was not her idea, nor would she act without Ressanda's approval. The baron is the one pressing for a marriage. Ressilka is only obeying her father, though I can say with certainty that Hallin was obeying Ressanda alone."

Scarlet winced. "You heard about that?"

"Of course."

Scarlet looked down at the engraved wood of the chair, tracing the patterns. "Everyone else knows, why not you?"

"It's my business to know, ser, even if I've been removed from my post. I'm still a Setna. The king speaks the truth when he says he cannot refuse Ressanda outright. Not now. Not when the realm needs Tebet's support. The king did make a promise, once."

"He promised that Ressilka would marry Cestimir or no man. Tell me how that figures into Liall taking a knee for her?

Imagination, I should think." Scarlet rose and began pacing the room. He did not seem to be able to keep still. "Why is he doing this to me? Does he hate me?"

"Baron Ressanda? He barely knows you."

"So did Vladei. That didn't stop him from trying to kill me," Scarlet said grimly, remembering that day in the forest on the Temple Road, the snow falling so thick he could barely see. Being herded into the ruins so that Cestimir could be murdered on ground the Rshani considered sacred, and Cestimir last words to him: *This way, I am free forever.*

"In my land, if a man tries to take another man's mate, he's an enemy," Scarlet said. "Doesn't that amount to Ressanda sending *me* a message with those damned horses? He wants me gone or dead. I can feel it."

"What Baron Ressanda wants is irrelevant." Jochi stood up and stepped in front of Scarlet to stop his pacing. His golden eyes were bright. "Ser Keriss, listen to me. The baron would not dare to lay hands on your life. He knows the king would destroy his entire family if he did so, and promises be damned. I think…" He hesitated and seemed to be choosing his words with care. "I think perhaps you are too close to the situation to see it clearly."

"All I can see is that Liall's kingdom wants him to take a wife, and me to take the first ship back to Byzantur. Or preferably a long drop off a tall pier and into the cold sea."

"Ser! This is not so. Everyone in the Nauhinir is fond of you. You are the adored of the king and there could be no kinder friend than you. Why do you say these hurtful things?"

Scarlet's chest was aching. "Because I'm scared, why

else? I don't think I can do what Liall wants this time, and I'm afraid I'll lose him for it. Isn't there another way?"

"The barons have not been sympathetic regarding the king's reluctance to marry and produce an heir. Their main concern is the stability of the realm. They care little for hearts, or whose may be broken."

"My heart isn't broken. Not yet, anyway. Like he said, they can't *make* him do it."

"But they can, ser."

Scarlet went very still. He could always rely on Jochi to tell as much of the truth as he was permitted to. One thing Jochi had never done was lie to him. "Tell me."

"They can put certain conditions on trade within Rshan, and claim that it is because the realm is unstable while there is no marriage and no heir. They can decline to give their aid in times of famine or want, or they can withhold information, or the use of their trading ships, or even refuse to send soldiers to guard the capital. They can do all manner of things that would take a month to explain to you. You must believe me: they are not powerless. The Council of Barons has always had a strong hand in the governing of Rshan. Unlike your Flower Prince, the voice of our king is not the voice of a deity."

"Maybe that should change."

Jochi tilted the same kind of look at him as Nevoi did when they sparred long-knives: measuring and cautious. "Were I you, I would take care in expressing such views openly. You know how close we came to civil war last year. If the king wages such a battle and loses, he will lose his head as well. And yours. Is that what you seek?"

"Of course not. I'm not a bloody fool, you know."

"Then heed me." Jochi put the book down and stared into Scarlet's eyes. "As much as I want to comfort you, I cannot reassure you on this matter. I cannot even agree with you. The king *must* have a wife and—very soon thereafter—an heir, and there is little if not nothing you can do to prevent it. You can delay it, yes, for years perhaps. But if you do, you also put the king in jeopardy. Quite aside from the politics and the danger, each day that the king sees your distress and pain and knows that he can do nothing to spare you, you hurt him."

Scarlet was resentful. "He hurt me enough when we came here, kept me locked away, told me nothing, shared nothing."

"He was *ashamed,*" Jochi said with patience. "He never wanted you to know the cause of his exile." His eyes narrowed. "Is that what this is about? I never took you for a vengeful person, ser. Looking back, even the king knows he was wrong to hide so much of his past from you, but you are the one hurting *him* now."

Scarlet frowned and crossed his arms. He would not have this monstrous unfairness turned back around on him. "I know where your loyalties rest, Jochi."

"I am loyal to the House of Camira-Druz. That includes you, ser. The king was wrong to lie to you and I have said so, but what's done is done. You cannot hold on to it forever. Do you really believe the king would choose to put a woman in his bed when he could have you?"

Scarlet's jaw tightened. "He was engaged to Shikhoza once. He isn't…" He faltered and his cheeks flushed. "He isn't like me… like that. He's bedded women before. He enjoys it. I can't do that."

Jochi's voice softened. "Is that what troubles you? You really don't know men very well, do you, ser? Listen then: Ressilka is beautiful, yes. And King Nazheradei has had a few female lovers in the past, but…" He held up his index finger meaningfully, "he's had more male lovers than women. Our king is known to prefer the touch of men. That fact puts Lady Ressilka at a distinct disadvantage that she will never be able to change or overcome. She's simply the wrong gender for him."

Scarlet blinked. "I hadn't thought…"

"You should. I hear that Ressilka rides with her father's men and learns the sword as they do, but she can't change who she is any more than you can grow taller."

Scarlet looked away. "And just how do you know so much about Liall's lovers?"

"Well, I do not know about the lovers he might have taken in your lands," Jochi demurred, "but here it is common knowledge. A royal court dearly loves gossip. Also, the king informed me."

Scarlet wondered how that subject might have come up. "I suppose you've talked to Ressilka, too?"

"Of course I have. The Lady Ressilka is not a close acquaintance, but I know her father well. She finds our king most pleasing."

Scarlet scowled. "You're trying to make me angry."

"I'm trying to make you see that you have weapons of your own in this battle, ser, if a battle it is. You have nothing to fear from a woman who simply cannot give the king what he most desires. She may become his wife and have his name, yes, but you will have his heart. Is that so little?"

A familiar ache throbbed in the middle of Scarlet's chest. "It's everything. But that's not how it will happen. She's beautiful and young and she can give Liall so much that I can't."

"A child."

He nodded, though Jochi hadn't guessed all of it. "I could fight for Liall if it was another man wanting him, but Ressilka's highborn and she's one of his people. If he marries her, she'll be the mother of his children. What will I be?" He returned to his chair and slumped in it, feeling almost ill. "You keep mentioning my rank, saying it's valuable, saying I should be aware of it. Well, what will my rank be when there's a queen in the Nauhinir again?"

Jochi hesitated, and Scarlet knew he had made a point.

"You should be telling all this to the king, ser, not to me," Jochi said. "If he knew your fears exactly, he could set your mind to rest."

"With words?" Scarlet said bitterly. "It's not words that count under the sheets. She'll share his bed and his children and his throne. You say your people accept me here in the palace. I know that, and I'm grateful. But as soon as she passes under the gates, I'll be the *lenilyn* foreigner again." He began to gnaw on a fingernail. Jochi was silent for so long that Scarlet looked up. "I'm right aren't I?"

Jochi stepped closer and pulled on Scarlet's wrist, tugging his finger away from his teeth.

"Don't chew your nails," he sighed. "It is a fact of nature, my young friend, though not a fair one, that blood often binds as closely as love. The king will not stop loving you if he marries the Lady Ressilka, but I can't promise you that he'll feel nothing for her in the years to come. I'll not lie to you; it's a lasting bond to marry and mate and produce children. Those are facts, unless the two to be paired are such enemies that profit or progeny are the only reasons they join. That's the kind of loveless marriage his mother had with Cestimir's father. Is that what you want for the king?"

"No," Scarlet said miserably. "And yes, damn it. I don't want him to love her."

"No two loves are exactly the same," Jochi said, his face set in lines of worry.

Scarlet shook his head, the shame in his heart burning. "No, you don't understand. I don't want him to love her in any way. At all. *I'm his mate!* Not her! We were meant for each other, Liall and me. At least that's what Deva teaches us. And if… if someone else can come in and change that, what does that say of us? What do we mean to each other if he can even *want* to bed someone else?"

Jochi looked troubled. "You are so young, and there is much that is unknown and unwritten about Hilurin. Rshani are quite different in many ways. But ser, are you saying that Hilurin do not bed with any but their mates? Ever?"

"We don't. I only heard tell of one or two Hilurin in my whole life who went astray of their vows, but some of us… we can't. Hilurin marriages are true bonds before the Goddess. They can only be broken by death." Scarlet felt a sudden dread. "I'm afraid that Liall may not feel the way I do.

He probably doesn't, and I never heard of any Rshani mating with a Hilurin before."

"It was done in our ancient past. We have many stories of it."

"But you don't know how it was, how they were bonded and how they lived?"

"Hundreds of texts have been lost over the centuries, especially those that contained any information about your people. We do not know a great deal about Hilurin abilities, either, because our ancestors purged that knowledge from history. Out of fear, I think." Jochi looked saddened. "What a loss."

Scarlet noted that Jochi refrained from naming his abilities *magic*. He had found that most Rshani either did not believe his magic was real or else they believed it was evil. He could do many things with his Gift now, much more than he could on the day he sailed from Byzantur with Liall.

"Watch," he said. He looked to the fire and made a gesture like scattering a handful of dust. The fire flared and babbled, sparks rising in a wave.

Jochi exhaled slowly, fascinated. "Where does such power come from?"

"From Deva, where else?" Scarlet murmured, looking at the innocent palm of his hand. "I can do so much more since I came to Rshan. The goddess must believe I need it, or why would she give it to me?"

"What else have you discovered you can do?" Jochi asked, very carefully.

"I can light fires from across a field," Scarlet confessed

absently. "Make a tree sprint through a year's growth in an eye-blink. I can close doors from across the room and cause the air to turn warm. Or cold, but there isn't much use for that here, is there? My magic has grown into something I don't recognize." He smiled a little. "Liall would call it elegant. To me, it feels like a caged lion I saw in Ankar once. It resents me and wants to get free of me. What if it just keeps growing?"

Jochi looked shaken. "We do not believe in gods. Not as you do. There were powers once in Rshan na Ostre, now faded beyond recognition. We have the Ancients, but we understand them."

"I don't. Melev healed me once. No curae could ever match him, not even a Hilurin. I've never seen power like that." Scarlet felt a shiver at the thought of Melev, who had saved him only to capture him later and attempt to use him for some dark purpose. He was certain that whatever Melev had planned to do to him in the temple ruins would have killed him, or left him such a ruin that not even Liall could love him. "Melev meant to cripple me, to steal my magic. He knew it would kill me, I think."

Jochi nodded agreement. "So I have guessed, but these are dark things. You should not think of Melev now, with all else that wounds your heart."

Scarlet gave him a wan smile. "Tactful. It's Liall who wounds my heart, but you can't speak ill of him because he's your king."

"And my friend."

"The friend who sacked you," Scarlet reminded. At least Liall had not sent Jochi away yet.

"He had cause. I know he loves you and would do anything to make this easier. The king has been careful to make inquiries about your happiness. He wishes you never to feel neglected. Or insulted," Jochi added. "In particular, he has made it known that any slight offered to his t'aishka would be considered a grave insult to the crown, and punishable. He wants only the best for you. He would spare you this hurt if he could."

"Maybe he can. He hasn't really tried to spare me from it so far," Scarlet said glumly. "We've had so little happiness together, why can he not *wait* even a little?"

"The king is wise enough to know there are some things he is not free to decline."

Scarlet flung his hand through the air as if to cast aside his aching heart with it. The fire answered in a roar, sending flames licking out toward the carpet. Jochi recoiled.

"Why can't she just look elsewhere for a man of her own?" Scarlet demanded. "She thought she might be Cestimir's queen, but does that mean she has to be queen or nothing? A man who's free to love her back might make her happier than a crown. Or maybe that isn't even her reason. Maybe she's in love with Liall. I wouldn't put it past her. Maybe I should never have come here!"

"I hope you don't mean that," came a deeper voice.

Jochi bowed low. Liall had entered the library as silent as a cat. He pushed the heavy cloak off his wide shoulders and dropped it into a chair. It was pale blue and had a high mantle of silver chased in elegant lines, and even in his anger Scarlet was admiring him, wanting him.

"Leave us, Jochi, please," Liall said.

Jochi bowed once more. "Sire."

When Jochi had gone, Liall stood by the fireplace, looking down into the flames. The fire crackled and threw orange shadows over his hard, handsome features, and Scarlet found himself aching all over again, worse than before.

She'll love him. Who wouldn't? And she won't step aside like some meek miss, not if there's a king, crown, and children to fight for. Not that one, no. She's a fighter, and she has all the odds on her side, even time. Time most especially.

"It usually sets a man's mind at ease to talk over his fears with his friends," Liall said. "I see it has not worked in this case. Please come here." He held out his hand, and Scarlet went to him.

"Why should words work when the facts haven't changed? Don't look at me like that. It isn't Jochi's fault. He tried. He isn't like most of your counselors. He tells me the truth and he admits it when I strike the nail on the head every now and then. I have plenty of good reasons to be afraid of this. How would you feel if I took a mate apart from you?"

Liall made a growling noise.

"There, you see?" Scarlet pointed a finger at Liall's nose. "You wouldn't like it if I shared my bed with someone else."

"I'd feel slightly more strongly about it than *dislike*." Liall's voice turned hard. "Why? Is there a man you have in mind?"

Scarlet summoned a bright, false smile. "Well, Tesk has always liked me. He painted my picture." He watched as Liall's dark face flooded with color. "But no."

"Then why in three hells did you bring it up?" Liall snarled in frustration.

"To see that look on your face, why else?"

"The Council of Barons—"

"I know, I know." Scarlet waved his hands. "Your barons want a woman for you and little princes to sit at your feet and inherit your throne, and I can't give you that, so they want me shoved aside so you can give Ressilka a big belly."

"Crudely put, but yes, that's the substance of it. Only I shall not allow you to be 'shoved aside'. You will not be supplanted or treated poorly. You will always be my t'aishka, always first in my heart and by my side. A queen will not sit at my right hand. You will. I wish blood and marriage were not such an issue when it comes to a throne, but wishing is futile. My barons want a *legitimate* prince of Camira-Druz, because my power and lineage secured equals their power secured. Does it make no difference at all to you that I have no choice?"

"Don't play stupid. It's the difference between a black sheep and a white one covered in soot. They're the same damn thing, just dressed up different."

Liall's expression grew bland. "Your colorful colloquialisms occasionally escape me, Scarlet. Perhaps less metaphor and more plain speech would be in order."

"Oh, go fuck yourself, you great prissy giant!" Scarlet shot back. "If you're going to start *that* with those mile-long words you know I don't understand then you can just pout here by your lonesome." He turned away.

"I am *not* pout… Scarlet, come back here!"

By the time he'd reached the door, Liall was ahead of him, blocking the way with his body. Liall leaned his back against the door and looked down at him.

"We are going to speak of this without you running away," he said solemnly. "I've let it go too long and now it's like a block of ice between us. It's pushing us apart and I cannot bear it. I don't enjoy forcing you, but you *will* hear me out this time."

"I've heard you!" Scarlet shouted, his heart thumping in fear. "I've heard you, I've heard Alexyin, I've heard Jochi, and I've heard you again and again. It's you who won't listen!"

"Alexyin?" Liall barked. "I did not give Alexyin leave to speak to you of these things. When did this happen?"

"It doesn't matter," Scarlet said quickly, aware that he had slipped up. Wouldn't Alexyin take that as proof that he had run to Liall with complaints? He was doing exactly what he said he wouldn't do. "I misspoke. I didn't speak with Alexyin about… about this."

Liall's eyes were dark, questioning. "You're lying to me," he said in wonder. "That's not like you in the least. Why are you lying to me, Scarlet?"

"Because you're not listening to what I'm really saying."

"I'm right here. I'm listening now," Liall pointed out with patience. "*Talk* to me, redbird."

Scarlet closed his eyes on a spasm of pain. He took a deep breath and bunched his fists. "How old are you?"

Liall's bows drew together in a little frown. "You know very well how old I am. I am in my eighth decade."

"You count time in decades," Scarlet said, ever so soft. "You live so long that some of you aren't even sure how old you are. How old was your mother when she died? How long had she ruled?" He swallowed in a dry throat and looked at the man he loved more than life. "My dad was thirty-six when he died, and he was old. His hands hurt so bad he couldn't even hold a rake. How old am I, Liall?"

Liall looked away, and Scarlet could see he did not like the path the conversation was taking. "You were seventeen when we met, or only just," Liall said uncomfortably. It wasn't the first time the difference in their ages had seemed to bother him, and it scandalized the Rshani court. "You're eighteen now, nineteen next summer. I don't see what this has to do with anything."

"You do see. You just won't face it," Scarlet said with a heavy sadness. *I have to tell him.* "I was so in love, and it was all so new and strange to me that I deliberately forgot the truth I've always known. I was selfish. I dreamed for a while, but that's over now." He touched Liall's cheek and looked straight into his eyes. "I'm not asking you never to marry, or never to have children. I didn't say that. I only asked you to *wait*."

It took a moment for it to sink in, and Scarlet's heart broke as he saw the truth hit his lover.

"Wait for you to *die?*" Liall said in dawning shock. "Is that what you're saying? That's what you want?"

"Yes."

Liall stared for a moment, his eyes wide with fear, then his old, confident, arrogant, infuriating self reasserted and he shook his head. "No. No, you're not going to die early like your kin did, Scarlet," he began, his voice dropping down into tones of calm. "I know your race is shorter-lived than mine, but the Hilurin you knew in Byzantur were peasants and farmers on the edge of the Bledlands. They suffered greatly, when the Aralyrin allowed them to live at all. I have no doubt that poverty and sickness contributed to their early demise. You're not going to die anytime soon."

"I have fifteen years," Scarlet said tiredly. He was so tired. "Twenty at the most. It used to seem like such a long time, but then I met you and… but I'm not asking you to wait until I'm gone. Before that, I'll be too old for you, and I won't object when you take someone younger. I'll understand then."

"Oh gods," Liall groaned. "Listen to yourself. Too old for me? You'll never be too old for me."

"I'll look like my father and you'll still be the same. That's what I mean by *too old*. You'll set me aside then, and you'll be right to." Scarlet marveled that he could say these things aloud. He had avoided doing it for so long, for Liall's sake as much as his own.

"I won't listen to this." Liall sounded like he was gasping for air. "It's not true." He turned away.

"Now who's running?" Scarlet's voice grew thin. "Don't leave, please."

Liall wrenched himself back from the door as if trying to tear himself in two. He pulled Scarlet into his arms roughly.

"Gods, why?" He moaned, wrapping his arms tight around Scarlet. "Why do we have so little time? It isn't right. It's not natural. You should live years beyond me, as honest and good as you are, not wither like a young tree in the cold. I can't…"

"Hush." Scarlet was struck with a sense of unreality. How odd that he should be the comforter now, when it had always been Liall before. Liall had always been stronger than him. *Perhaps not in this*, he thought. Liall desired to control everything around him, on his terms. He was a wolf wherever he went, forever snapping at the universe to align with his will.

"This cannot happen," Liall whispered.

Scarlet had never heard him sound so scared. "It will, and you have to live with it. What else can you do?"

"What can I do?" Liall echoed softly, his hands restless as he petted Scarlet's hair, and Scarlet felt the slight tremble in his fingers. "What can I do? I must do something… I must do something…"

"I cannot lose you," Liall repeated over and over again as he held him in their bed, after they had loved. Though the sun never set now, the heavy casements were closed, sealing out the light. The only illumination was the flickering fire, stoked with sweet woods that burned with an aroma almost like perfume.

According to the marks on the candle, it was very late at night. The Nauhinir was quiet and Liall's bare skin was warm against his side.

"All life is filled with loss," Scarlet whispered against Liall's chest, his fingers stroking the deep amber of his lover's skin. "If we're lucky and good, there's some love in there, too. I think I love you enough for ten lifetimes."

Liall hugged him tighter. "Ten lifetimes wouldn't be enough. I won't accept losing you."

"What else can you do?"

Liall looked down at him. His long hand brushed Scarlet's hair away from his temples, and Scarlet saw the steely determination on his features.

"I don't know that I can do anything, but I'm not a man who accepts defeat easily. You should know that. There are curaes in Rshan unlike any you have in Byzantur, very wise and learned men. For all we know, the early deaths of your people may be from some sickness of the blood or foreign malady that no one has investigated yet, something endemic to Byzantur but unknown here. You forget: the Hilurin are not *from* Byzantur. Not originally. Rshan is your true land. Don't look cross with me, I'm speaking the truth. The Aralyrin live much longer than you, yes? And you can hardly tell some of them from a pure Hilurin."

"But that's just because—"

"No, no arguments. For now, put thoughts of death from your mind. And forget Ressilka, too. The barons can go hang."

Scarlet sighed. "I'm too selfish to protest. I can't pretend I want you to have her, not now. Even when I'm gone, I suspect I'll resent it."

"You're not going anywhere."

Scarlet saw the iron in Liall's pale blue eyes, and he felt cold. What could Liall possibly do to change nature? Hilurin were short-lived. There were reasons for that, he was sure, though they were known only to Deva. His people cherished life more because of it. They were closer to the earth and closer to the gods for it. They married young, prized their children, and risked their scant time in the world much less on wandering and chance. Few Hilurin were what anyone could call adventurous, and when they were, they were branded with suspicion like Scarlet had been. Men with the Wilding were thought to be poor mates and providers.

Well, perhaps he was no fit mate for a woman, but he had been a good one to Liall. It bothered him that he seemed to be failing in that duty now. *A good mate would want children for his beloved,* he decided. *I should want to see him content and happy at his fireside, with plump children at his feet. Instead, I just want him to take me hunting or on a long journey. I'd even be happy to go to sea again.*

"I wish we could leave," he sighed, pressing a kiss to Liall's bronze throat. "I wish we could travel the roads again, even just for a little while."

Liall was silent for a moment. "Perhaps we can," he said. "Don't roll your pretty black eyes at me, ser Impertinence. It's not an empty promise, though you may not like where we go."

Scarlet thought he heard something in that. "Has something happened?"

"Old business. The tribesmen in the north are looting and burning again. It has stirred some debate about what precisely is to be done." Liall paused. "I've called a baron's council to discuss the matter."

It was never as easy as Liall made it sound. If he said there was a problem, that meant there had already been blood. "So there will be a battle?"

"More than one, I suspect. It's nothing new, love. There were battles in your land, too."

"Hilurin don't attack their own people," Scarlet murmured unhappily. "You have a fine kingdom here. Your people are healthy and well fed, and there are no slaves or any great want. Why do you fight among each other so much?"

"It's our nature, I think. We may despise outlanders, but we tolerate each other little better. We are territorial and jealous and we lust for power. There are nations like that in the south, too."

"Yes, the Minh," Scarlet said. "You're not like the Minh at all."

"Don't be too sure. Most powerful nations have more in common that you like to think about. We do not keep slaves, true, but we take what we want on the seas. We don't even call that piracy, just keeping our waters safe. Any ship that comes near Rshan without letters of commission from the crown will be set upon and seized. And some, my little pedlar, don't even wait for the ships to come that close. You forget: Rshani don't feel that outlanders have souls. When a Rshani warrior kills a Morturii or a Minh, they don't believe they're killing a true person, merely something with the shape of a person."

"You don't believe that."

"I do not, no. I don't think I ever did. Neither did

Cestimir, or my lady mother. But I am not your common Rshani, and I've lived outside of these lands much longer than I've lived in them."

Scarlet sighed against Liall's skin. "I hate that kind of thinking. I wish you wouldn't keep reminding me."

Liall rubbed Scarlet's back in small circles. "I have to keep reminding you," he said. "You can't get too comfortable in your safety here, redbird. My court may love you, but there will always be men who don't."

Scarlet nearly purred and threw a leg over Liall's hips, snuggling closer. "Well, they're not here, are they?"

"They may come here."

Scarlet sensed a message in that. He looked up. "Did… are they here? She is, isn't she? Here in the palace. Lady Ressilka."

"No, no. Set your mind at ease." Liall kissed Scarlet's cheek and whispered, *"I'm sorry, my love,"* against his skin.

Scarlet put his head back down on Liall's chest. "I've lost track; what exactly are you apologizing for?"

"For hurting you. I shouldn't have pushed you so hard to agree to something that is against your nature."

Scarlet pulled away from Liall's embrace and sat up. "Can you do it? Refuse her, I mean. Is it possible?"

Liall rubbed his jaw. He looked very tired. "Perhaps. Not bluntly, and certainly not now. But perhaps a way can be found where Ressanda is satisfied."

"Not Ressilka?"

"This was never about her. Royal marriages are seldom about what the bride and groom want. I don't know if the girl likes me or hates me or wishes me quartered in a gibbet cage. I've only spoken to her once."

Scarlet swallowed hard and felt his eyes stinging. "For however long you manage to delay it, thank you."

"You misunderstand me."

For a moment, Scarlet was afraid. "How?"

"Putting a hook in a bear's mouth is a dangerous undertaking. I can lure the baron and play him for time, but at some point the game will end and he'll know he's been maneuvered. When he realizes that, he might withdraw his offer of Ressilka's hand. That's when the game becomes deadly."

"A game. Is that what a crown really is?"

"Depend on it."

"Liall, I don't want you to be childless and alone after I'm gone."

Liall mussed Scarlet's hair fondly. "Fool. You're not going anywhere. You're going to stay with me until I'm old and gray and you beg me to stop trying to make love to you, because I'm wrinkled and have no teeth left and I'm too ugly to fuck."

"Now you're just making fun of me," Scarlet said crossly, reaching for the sheet to pull around his nakedness.

Liall jerked the sheet away. "Stop that, I like to look at you. And I'm not joking. We're going to be old men together, tottering our way to the throne room with servants holding our hands to keep us from getting lost."

"That's impossible."

"Nothing is impossible that men can dream. I thought magic was impossible, didn't I? I knew it as sure as I knew what direction the sun rose and the color of my eyes. Well, I was wrong. If I was wrong about magic, then it follows I may have been wrong about the gods, too. Your Deva, for instance."

"*You* believe in the goddess, now?" Scarlet couldn't hide the doubt in his voice.

Liall's smile was wry. "Belief has always been a fraught word for me. It's not in *my* nature to believe in what I can't see or touch. I believe in fire, for example. If I should ever doubt it, sticking my hand in a pile of coals would neatly reaffirm my faith. A god is more difficult. Where is my measure for taking stock of a god? Strangely, it's you."

"Me?" Scarlet didn't like the sound of that. "Talk about plowing the wrong field. I'm no priest!"

"No, you're not," Liall agreed. "You're closer to being a holy man than any priest I've ever known."

Scarlet gaped. "Oh, for Deva's sake!" He pushed Liall's leg with his foot and clambered out of the bed. The damn thing was so deep and wide that he could never manage getting out of it gracefully. It was a sea of a bed. *And Liall the titan of the waters.* The thought made him laugh aloud. "I've fought, cursed, blasphemed, gambled, drank, disobeyed my parents, and taken a man for a lover. I don't know how the goddess feels about the last but I'm positive she disapproves of everything else. Hell's teeth, where can you find anything *holy* in all that?"

Liall propped himself up on an elbow and smiled from the ocean of sheets and furs; a long, lean god carved from golden oak. Scarlet's throat went tight just looking. *Holy? He must be mad. There are better behaved bhoros houses than the way we carry on sometimes.*

"You have your magic." Liall smiled. "The goddess didn't take it from you, so she must not be too displeased by all your grievous *transgressions.*" He rolled the word off his tongue and patted the pillow next to him. "Come back, *iaresh*, and let's see how far we can presume celestial forbearance."

"I don't know what that means," Scarlet said, aware that they were only bantering now, and also fully aware that Liall was teasing and trying to entice him to more lovemaking. *And making me rise like a stallion scenting a mare in season.*

"Iaresh means beauty. For the rest… no matter. You love me," Liall went on, smiling confidently. "A man who—as I've informed you many, many times—is quite unworthy of your love on a godlike scale. Thus, there are two miracles for you. We're due a third."

"Stark mad, that's what you are," Scarlet pronounced, his hands on his naked hips. "Moonstruck, madcap, and village fool, all in one gigantic lump of a want-wit who needs to shut up!" He grabbed a pillow and hurled it at Liall's head.

Liall declined to duck. The pillow smacked him full on the nose.

"Oops."

Scarlet yelped and darted across the room when he discovered just how fast the king could move when motivated. "Accident! Accident!" he protested, laughing and taking cover behind a couch.

"Striking your king is no accident." Liall grinned.

"It was only a pillow!"

"A crime is a crime." Liall caught him and held him close to his chest. "And penalty is still required," he breathed, his mouth on Scarlet's cheek, his hands sliding low to cup and fondle.

Scarlet felt his knees go weak. "Oh? Best get to it, then. You know how we criminals hate waiting to be tortured."

Liall lifted him in his arms and hauled him back to the bed.

By the time the coals of the fire had died out completely, Scarlet was flopped across Liall's body like a rag doll. Liall toyed lazily with Scarlet's hair, curling it around his fingers.

"You know," Scarlet murmured thoughtfully, "if I'm to have a life here in Rshan, I'll need to have some manner of work."

Liall grunted, his eyes half-closed to slits of pale blue that watched intently. The room was dark, every shape outlined in silver and gray to keen Hilurin sight.

"Are you not content to be employed merely as the king's bed-toy?"

Scarlet tried to swat him and missed, then gave up the effort. It was too hard to move anyway. "Well, it's fine for the nights," he answered. "Not that there are any right now. But I've always worked for my bread. It's strange to be given everything and have to *do* nothing. That's not what Scaja raised me to be."

"And here I am thinking I've been giving you plenty to do. I've been remiss. Wake me in an hour and I'll see to it."

"Ha. I won't be sitting down for dinner as it is, thank you," Scarlet retorted, and grinned when Liall's chest and belly shook with silent laughter under him. "I'm serious, *stop* laughing, you fool." He nipped one of Liall's nipples with gentle teeth. "I'm not kidding. I need work to keep my hands and head busy. I'm used to an active life, you know. Traveling. Fighting. Killing soldiers. That sort of thing. All this bed-work will make me soft."

Liall's fingers trailed up his spine. Scarlet wriggled in ticklish protest. "You're already quite soft. Always were."

Scarlet had not known that. He'd never thought of it, really: how he would compare to the lovers Liall had known before. "Is it so?"

Liall nodded. "Soft as the new leaf of a snowy rose."

"Oh, and poetry, too. I think you're the one who's gone soft, but in the head."

"Rather more south, I think." Liall took Scarlet's hand and pushed it down. "You could remedy that for me."

"Again? Gods below, you're insane. I'm going to sleep."

Liall chuckled again and tugged Scarlet until he was on the pillows beside him. "All right then, let's talk about it. What kind of work did you have in mind?"

Scarlet hesitated, afraid Liall would think him silly. He reached up and pushed Liall's hair back from his face. Since they had come to Rshan, Liall had begun to let his hair grow longer, as was the custom. Jochi had fine, silken hair to the small of his back, and Alexyin's mane of white hair, unbraided, fell nearly to his knees. Liall's hung to his shoulders and was merely shaggy now, and though he had begun to complain of the nuisance of it, he had not cut it.

"I've always wanted to try smithing," Scarlet said, tracing his finger down the bridge of Liall's fine nose.

"You mean with a forge?"

"No, with a shank of mutton, want-wit. Of course with a forge. And tongs and hammers and all sorts of things that turn a piece of iron into a blade."

Liall frowned. "You want to learn to make swords?"

"I can already make them. Well, a little anyway. I used to hang around the forge in Lysia where my father bought horseshoes. The smith used to give me metal to play with, and I had a little hammer. The handle was broken off but it was just right for my hand. I used to pretend I was hammering armor to ride off to battle, maybe to fight for the Flower Prince."

An odd note touched Liall's voice. "You wanted to be a soldier?"

"Don't all little boys want to be soldiers? I grew out of it. Anyway, there was a forge in Ankar, too, across the souk from Masdren's shop. The smith was named Jao, which is a funny name for a Morturii. It means 'ouch'."

Liall chuckled. "I like this story. Go on."

"I worked at Jao's forge betimes, picking up some extra coppers. He taught me some, but I always wanted to learn more. He said learning the science of metal was difficult, but all the rest was just long practice and hard work, which I'd have to apprentice with him to really master. And then," he sighed, "well, you know what then." Lysia was burned and everyone driven out or dead. He was silent for a moment, thinking. "My sister's husband is a blacksmith, too."

Liall nodded. "Shansi. I remember. It's a good trade in Byzantur, especially for Hilurin, who are so clever with their hands."

"Scaja had a way with carving wood and painting, and Linhona could embroider better than the queen's maids in Morturii."

"Clever hands, all of you," Liall repeated. He raised Scarlet's hand—the narrow left one with the missing finger—to his mouth and kissed it. "But I don't know if I want these hands near molten iron. Many accidents happen with forges, love, and this hand in particular could be a liability to you."

"My hand is fine," Scarlet said steadily. "I've plowed with it and ridden and traveled from Ankar to Omara and even killed a man with this hand. There's nothing wrong with my hands."

"Save that they are very small. I shudder to think of them near a forge fire."

"You could find someone to teach me. Rshani smiths are the some of the best I've seen in the world," Scarlet coaxed, knowing he had no chance of it without Liall's help. There wasn't a tradesman in the kingdom who would take him on as apprentice without the king's approval, even if it wasn't dangerous.

Liall's frown darkened. "You'd have to promise to be

very careful," he warned. "And—"

"Thank you," Scarlet said quickly, kissing his cheek.

"*And* if it becomes no longer safe, you have to stop," Liall finished.

"Fire burns, steel melts. How could blacksmithing become any more unsafe than it already is?"

"I don't know. A thousand reasons, and not all of them having to do with smithing. All I can promise is to find a man from whom you can learn. Do you think I like to see you mired up or bored? There are only so many rabbits to hunt, and you haven't taken to reading like I thought you might."

"Too slow," Scarlet muttered resentfully. "Every word in those books is a boulder, and I'm like a tortoise bumbling over those rocks one by one. I'd rather be out *doing* rather than sitting down and reading what someone else has done."

"You could always read standing up."

Scarlet pinched him and watched the grin spread over Liall's face in the darkness. "What's writ about riding a horse isn't the same as riding one. Life isn't for watching. If I can't travel where I will, then I want to be a *part* of the life around me, not just hear about it. I've never been much of a layabout, but if I sit on my arse much longer it will be too big even for you."

Liall choked on laughter.

"You know what I mean," Scarlet said crossly. "I'm not ready to be idle like an old grandfather. Not yet."

"You will not be. I swear it," Liall vowed, laughing as he drew the covers and furs up over them. "I will begin the search tomorrow. But now, we really do have to sleep. My life just became immeasurably more complicated."

Scarlet was silent for a moment as they settled into the bed comfortably. "Because of me," he added softly.

Liall's arm was tight around his waist and their bodies were warm where they pressed together.

"Only in part," he said. "When the alternative is not having brought you to Rshan at all, I count my blessings. We knew life would not be easy for us here, redbird."

"In my wildest daydreaming, I never thought I'd end up here, with you. Scaja used to say my head was in the clouds, and that I had too many grand notions about myself, but I only ever wanted a simple life."

Scarlet drifted off to sleep, listening to the steady thump of Liall's heart. *A simple life,* was his last thought before mist closed around his mind and he dreamed of a land so cold it froze the lungs, and of a wall of fog that rose up around an immense tower shaped like a wheel.

Fading Dreams

Ulan was an eerie copy of Melev. Liall could tell one Ancient's features from another only with long familiarity of their race, and he did not know Ulan very well. For a short time in his childhood, Ulan had been his teacher and protector, but the memory was foggy within him.

Girded about Ulan's lanky, towering frame was a simple linen tunic knotted with a leather cord, leaving his flat, broad feet and ropy arms bare. His eyes were as large as apricots and as colorless as moonstones, and his skin was like a wind-blasted oak, reddish-amber and rough. His nose was hooked, his jaw like a block of wood, and each knotty finger of his plate-sized hands had an extra joint that the Rshani lacked. An Ancient standing very still in a forest could be mistaken for a bare tree in winter.

Liall knew that some trees in the deep forests beyond the Greatrift actually *were* dormant Ancients, but it took a deliberate effort of will for them to shift to such a latent state, and once it was done they must remain so for many years. Whenever he witnessed an Ancient in motion, he could sense the burning life within them, and how very alien they were.

Ulan stood waiting in Liall's solar, his body a broad, rough scrawl against the elegant folds of a tapestry. He bowed his head slightly: as close to homage as any Ancient would ever render to a Rshani, royal or no. "King Nazheradei, the wolf."

Liall returned the bow with a wry smile. There were two

kinds of power in the room. One stemmed from the realm where a king ruled the lives of other men with simplicity and directness. The other ruled from a place of ice and legend that no mortal Rshani could ever fully understand.

"Not a very complimentary address, is it?" Liall said. "Perhaps they should have called me the Bear when I was in Byzantur. It would have translated so much better." Wolves were considered scavengers and pests in Rshan, not the romantic mountain beasts of the Southern Continent; the land that Rshani crudely called *Kalaslyn.* In more polite moments, they referred to it as the Brown Lands or just Outland, if they spoke of it at all.

"Wolves have their place. Bears have their place," Ulan said.

The deep rumble that his vocal chords produced seemed to sink into the timber beneath Liall's boots and vibrate.

"Ah, but it's finding that place that matters, yes?" Liall answered. "Here, a wolf is scorned and the snow bear is honored. I might as well have been named for the bat or dragonfly for all the respect *wolf* lends me here." He motioned to the banner of Camira-Druz on the wall: scrolling lines of silver across a field of blue. Nearby was the shield of Camira-Druz with its lumbering white snow bear and golden star shining above. The eyes of the bear created two more golden stars below; a symbol of the Longwalker constellation that winked pale and lonely over the horizon of Rshan na Ostre during the dark winter.

The great lamps of Ulan's eyes followed the direction Liall indicated. "We have heard that your t'aishka was blooded by the bear."

"That part is true," Liall said carefully. He was not fond of recalling that fateful hunt last winter, when Scarlet had been injured and nearly crushed by the charging snow bear, and Vladei had been revealed for the traitor he was.

"The bear perished by your t'aishka's hand. *Sun hinir,* the great hunter of the ice, slain by so small a hand." Ulan looked at his own palm and moved his fingers reflexively. "We hear that our Rshani scions name him Keriss, meaning the flame flower. We are very curious to hear more of *Scarlet* of Lysia."

Liall felt the hairs on the back of his neck rise. "Is my t'aishka welcome in the eyes of the Ancients?"

Ulan nodded his great head. "More than welcome. Ten thousand welcomes. Our races have been sundered too long. It is the old way."

Melev had said the same, and Melev had also claimed that Scarlet was welcome. The truth was that Melev had considered Scarlet an object, a thing to be used to achieve a goal, as evidenced by the way he had kidnapped Scarlet and aided in the murder of Cestimir.

Liall sat down, never taking his eyes off the Ancient. Ulan stared back at him without blinking. It was difficult not to be cowed by such eyes. Like Melev, Ulan was intensely interested in all things Hilurin, or *Anlyribeth* as they had been known in Rshan more than an age ago. Deliberately, Liall had kept the details of Melev's treachery under wraps.

"The old way," Liall mused. "Very few know how far Melev went, either to satisfy his interest in Scarlet's magic or his own personal quest for power."

"I know."

Liall nodded. "And I am afraid your curiosity runs along similar lines, and carries with it the same quest for the lost knowledge of the Shining Ones."

Ulan was silent. His eyes were steady, giving Liall nothing.

Liall tried a new tack. "That the Ancients have kept the Rshani people ignorant of the true nature of the relationship between the Anlyribeth and the Shining Ones is deeply disturbing to me."

After a moment, Ulan nodded again. "You know of these matters?"

"I've put it together, more or less. Most wouldn't, but I've been surrounded by Setna since I was a child, and I dwelled in Kalaslyn for many years. The Hilurin haven't changed much, have they?"

"They had no need," Ulan rumbled. "They were complete. Perfect. It was our ancestors who were lacking. We needed the magic of the Anlyribeth to survive. We were their channels, they were the source. Or, no…" Ulan swung his head from side to side in negation. "No, not the source."

Liall could not recall ever witnessing an Ancient correct himself. He leaned forward. "Then who… *what* is this source?"

Ulan made a sound in his throat like a wave pounding a shore. Liall frowned. Ulan made the noise again, and Liall realized it was a word.

He had no hope of reproducing that sound. "What does it mean?"

"Deva."

Liall snorted. "You want me to believe in the legends of the Flower Prince? That the goddess favors the Hilurin, speaks to them, protects them and gives them magic?"

"Their magic is of *Her*. She deeded it to them before She dispersed."

Deeded. It seemed an odd choice of phrase, as did *dispersed*. "It was a gift?"

Ulan nodded. "The Gift. The Anlyribeth speak the truth."

"I've found they rarely lie."

Magic. Liall did not trust it, and he was deeply suspicious whenever the topic was mentioned. Because Scarlet was new to the jaded court and such a novelty to them, the topic came up quite often within Liall's hearing, especially since Scarlet had chosen a very public way to reveal his magic. Now everyone knew, and everyone was curious about what more there was to know, how far the mysteries went. It was a danger.

Liall decided to maneuver from a new direction. "You know of the revolt in the north, of Magur and what happened there."

Ulan nodded slowly, as if he expected this change of topic. He turned his gaze to the casement and looked at the land spreading out beyond. "Many deaths. Vladei brother-prince sought to use the Ava Thule in his bid for the throne. Melev helped him."

"And so they're all dead, as it should be," Liall said. "The last great incursion between the Rshani and the Ava Thule was the Tribeland campaigns. Before Magur, decades had passed without a whisper of them. My people hoped they had all perished, swallowed up by the winds beyond the Greatrift. The freeriders knew they were still sheltering in the foothills of Magur, but that information never seemed to reach the south." He watched Ulan, but could read nothing from him. "Until the revolt. Then there was no more pretending."

Ulan splayed a large hand against the glass, as if seeking the cold outside.

"How could you do it? How could *you* permit those savages inside the temple mountain?"

Ulan was unmoved. "Wars are things of men. They do not last. Only the sky lasts, and the suns that wheel in the heavens, and the language of stars. It is not our business to deal death and swing swords."

"Then it's not your business to take sides, either."

"We have taken no side. The generations of mortals rise and fall like wheat. Fissures open in the land. Mountains collapse. Ice melts. Only we endure."

"You've sheltered our enemies," Liall accused. "Given them food and a safe haven to gather and breed more rebellion."

"When brothers fight and a father comforts one of his injured sons, is that taking sides as well?"

"They're not children," Liall said in disgust. "You know what they're capable of. You know what they've *done*. We've shown them mercy before. We always harbored hope that the Tribelands would eventually bow to the rule of the crown, as they should have from the beginning. It's been too long now and their nature has changed beyond recognition. Since the days of Ramung, they've ravaged the northern lands, preying on outlying settlements, murdering travelers, stealing from the very cradles of the village folk to swell their numbers. They're animals, answering to no law, respecting no boundaries, living like wild beasts of the glacier and cave. Their numbers have grown great and the Ancients have not only kept their secret, but now you aid them against us."

"How have we aided them?"

"You allowed them to enter Ged Fanorl."

Ulan shook his head in his slow and plodding way. "They found the entrance to the temple mountain and unlocked her secrets. We did not help them. We simply did not prevent." The Ancient's lassitude was deceptive. Liall knew that Ulan was capable of moving faster than sight if he chose to. The fey ancestor-race of the Rshani were unknowable. It would be perilous to mistake either their motives or their capabilities. A misstep either way could prove disastrous.

Liall decided honesty was best. He doubted that he could hide anything from Ulan anyway. "We will make war against the Ava Thule. It's already begun. You knew that might happen one day, if your secret got out."

Ulan's voice turned deeper with displeasure. "It was *you* who opened that door, king."

Liall's jaw clenched. He had kept the secret nearly all his life, but now silence was a hazard at best, and treason if his subjects choose to see it that way. "I had to. The temple mountain is sacred to all Rshani, and your friends grew bold, attacking deeper inside our lands. It was only a matter of time before the truth broke. If I had not done this, the monarchy would have been destroyed. It might still be, no matter what I choose."

Ulan dropped his hand from the glass. "If the Ava Thule are not Rshani, then what are they? Where do you imagine they sprang from, if not the Shining Ones?" He made a discontented noise like a chair sliding on wood.

"Could it be that you wanted them to open the mountain *for* you?" Liall pressed. Ulan was not required to answer him at all. An Ancient could arrive in Nau Karmun clad in a ragged tunic and demand an audience with the king at once, and not only be tolerated, but venerated. He had nothing to pressure Ulan with.

To his surprise, Ulan's chin rose and his eyes seemed to burn like sunlight glinting off a shard of ice. "Many years ago, they found the way inside. Now the Ava Thule have learned of the return of the Anlyribeth. Many have journeyed to the temple mountain," he rumbled. "*Many.* A pilgrimage. They said they would open the temple and unlock the secrets of the hidden power, the lost magic. We have let the mountain rest these thousands of years. Now, one of *them* has returned of his own will. Not a captive, not a slave or subject, but one driven by love. The Ava Thule say it is but the beginning. More will follow. It is time to wake the magic."

Liall's heart clenched. Scarlet had spoken with him before about the Creatrix, said that his deadly encounter with Melev had shown him the location of the ancient magic of the Shining Ones.

"I won't allow you to harm Scarlet. I won't allow *them* to. My mother refrained from annihilating the Ava Thule *on your word.* She let the fleas live for your sake, for the Ancients and for the blood we share with them, but no more."

"You would kill them all?"

"They killed themselves when they entered Ged Fanorl," Liall answered. "I fought in the Tribelands campaigns when I was young. We hunted and burned them out of our lands. We drove them beyond the borders of Uzna and into the ice before the Ancients asked us to stop. You had never asked anything of us before."

"You showed mercy."

"We showed weakness. Why were you so merciful? Do you know what the Ava Thule really are?" Liall was angry now, remembering those battles, the atrocities he had witnessed. He stood up and paced the room. "If you had seen for yourself what they did, you would not call them your sons. They kill to win their mates. They cast their dead into pits with no burial, and they expose their female infants on the hillsides. Why waste food on raising a female when they can simply steal one of breeding age? The boy-children are tied arm-to-arm and made to fight over food and shelter, or for girls barely old enough to bleed. And they do worse. Much worse. Nothing grows in the North but mushrooms and lichen. The Ava Thule's knowledge of growing is gone, and they don't hunt the village-lands only to steal carrots and sheep and women. They have hunted men as *food.*"

Ulan was eerily still. "The wolf pack is not very different from what you describe. It is primal necessity, what they have become. They live according to the dictates of their environment."

"Even wolves don't cannibalize their own. I'm done trying to harry them back into the wastes, or trying to reason with you." Liall took a deep breath. "I won't wait until these animals are howling at our door before I act. I'm taking the army north to wipe them out."

Ulan made a burbling sound. It took Liall several seconds to recognize it as laughter.

"You do not make this war only to protect your people, scion of the Camira-Druz. Your crown *needs* a war."

"Fair enough," Liall grated out. "But it changes nothing. All I have said of them is true, and they are no less a threat for the happy convenience of timing. Warn them or not as you will, but we are coming, and Ged Fanorl will be cleansed."

He looked at Ulan, trying to gauge his reaction. It was difficult to measure even the strongest emotions when dealing with an Ancient. Their dark, broad faces at times seemed to be carved from solid wood. Scarlet, being a Hilurin with an open nature that concealed almost nothing, complained that Liall was secretive. If only Scarlet knew. Liall feared that Ulan could read him as easily as he read Scarlet's moods.

Ulan appeared to be looking *through* him. Liall wanted to shiver. He had the same feeling as when Scarlet used his magic; a sense of unreality jarring his perception of the world. Did Ulan have a similar magic that allowed him to read minds?

Ulan put one flat foot forward and advanced a step. "There is much you must see, much for you to learn before you reach Ged Fanorl, and there is little time. The channel must have a doorway, the link must be completed."

"I don't understand what that means." *Riddles, always riddles!*

"You will."

"And I don't appreciate your gods-cursed inscrutability!"

Ulan's wide mouth stretched further in a rare smile. "Even gentle creatures turn predator when they hunger, and into scavengers when starving. You call it abomination, but you have never starved as the Ava Thule have starved. Your fingers and toes have not turned black. The cold has not frozen your mate as she slept, or your babes in their cradles. In the elder times, when the long cold came and night lay on the land like a sickness, I saw worse than the deeds of the Ava Thule, King Nazheradei."

"You shall not see it again," Liall vowed.

"And what if I said that the thing you desire above all else will be given to you freely by your enemies, the Ava Thule, from what they have discovered inside Ged Fanorl?" Ulan paused and looked down on him. "Your t'aishka is fragile."

Liall stiffened. "If you dare threaten him…"

"I would not waste breath threatening you." Ulan loomed and his voice seemed to shudder the walls. "What need have I to threaten? If I meant the Anlyribeth harm I could root him from the stone of this castle and crush him with my own hands, and neither you nor all your spears could prevent me. This you know."

Liall held his tongue, though his vision had begun to narrow in a long tunnel focusing on Ulan. *Berserker rage*, he thought, and willed it back so hard that spots swam before his eyes. He forced himself to wait before speaking, to breathe, to grip the edge of a chair to steady himself. "You will not do that."

"Not I, no. Death will take a different form for your t'aishka. Forty summers, is it? Less, if their lives are hard. Even if you coddled him in a golden cage until he sickened of it, you will still live centuries beyond his span."

Liall felt like the floor was sinking beneath him. It was true. *Surely I've not lived all my adult life without love, only to find it and lose it in a handful of years? I cannot have come this far only to watch my love die before his time and leave me with only old age to endure alone. Fate is not that cruel.*

Ulan waited like a statue: unknowable, unreadable.

Liall swallowed hard. "I will not speak of this," he said hoarsely.

Ulan advanced toward him again. "He will not remain as he is for long. You will bury an old man in less than two decades," he said pitilessly. "And before that time, his love for you will turn bitter and rancid when he continues to age and you do not, when the fire of his life burns down and yours remains vital and strong. He will never see you in your age, but you will see him wither day by day, year by swift year, until you cannot bear to look at him."

Liall could hear Ulan's breath, heavy and slow. "Stop."

"As he knows you will. Scarlet is wiser than you in this. That is why your lover flees from you already, why his temper grows short and his eyes grow desperate. He will die, and you will live on."

"Enough!"

"He will do worse than die, Nazheradei. He will try to leave you. And when you do not permit that, when you keep him captive against his will, he will hate you for it. *Scarlet will grow to hate you.*"

Liall's arm swept out and he drew his knife. *"Stop!"* He held the blade in a trembling fist. "I will cut your heart out if you do not stop."

Ulan reached for him.

It was like the touch of something natural, but not living, the limb of a tree or a wall of rock. Ulan's hand came down on Liall's shoulder and the world wavered and undulated like a frond of seaweed beneath the water. Then it was gone.

Ulan's mind was cold, filled with ice and hoarfrost in every breath. Liall's body grew cold with it and seemed to freeze and blow away like snow. He was bodiless, a thought on the wind, a skirl of mist, then the world coalesced. Before him was an expanse of ice as far as he could see. The very air seemed to glow like a milky diamond. Clouds floated above the land, blanketing it. In the distance was a tower shaped like a monstrous wheel made of stone and iron. The ground hummed beneath his feet in a rhythmic thumping.

The Blackmoat. How can I be here?

The tower of the Setna loomed above them, casting no shadow. Thousands of years old, it was a monument to the genius and power of the Ancients. Their earliest makers had crafted the wheel, and crafted, too, its purpose. Liall could hear the slow, muffled *boom* of each impact deep into the earth, and as he watched the wheel turned and one grinding, metallic *clack* echoed over the glacier like an explosion. The entire immense structure rotated a fraction of a turn.

The Setna were the inheritors of the Ancient's knowledge. Only they could operate the wheel designed by the Red King. Only they knew how to refine the black sludge that came from deep beneath the ice, so that the fuel could be burned in their lamps and homes and heat the greenhouses that fed them through the lean months. The fuel was trade with foreign lands, food, gold, and all manner of goods in abundance. The Blackmoat was the grand wealth of Rshan na Ostre, its value almost immeasurable.

Liall seemed to float toward the tower, his body no more than a snowflake pushed by the wind, then he was inside it, in a room painted with bright colors on the walls and vivid woven rugs on the floor. Painted birds flitted over the walls, and patterns of vines and leaves framed the window. It was a Hilurin room.

A padded chair faced the window, and hanging on the wall above the flickering hearth was the likeness of Scarlet that Tesk had painted. Liall stared at it. Scarlet had borrowed Liall's necklace of copper coins for the sitting, the necklace that otherwise never left his possession. Scarlet's pedlar's coat was deep red. Light glinted off his black hair and his flawless skin glowed.

So beautiful, Liall thought tenderly, his heart rising. *So rare and fine, and so unaware of what a treasure he is.*

"Who's there?"

The voice was cracked and quavering. Liall realized a small man was seated in the chair. A blanket covered his legs, and wispy white hair haloed his skull.

Liall swallowed. "I'm… Nazheradei." He had forgotten his wolf name. It was lost somewhere, along with the friends he had known then, so long ago. Peysho, Kio, old Dira. Lost. Far away. Probably dead.

"Liall?"

He knew that voice. "No," he whispered. The voice was wrong. It was old and feeble, dry as a weathered bone. *It can't be.*

Liall knelt by the chair and made himself look. "Scarlet?" *Why is Scarlet at the Blackmoat? This room looks like his father's home, but no… Lysia was burned.*

The shrunken old man turned his face away. "I told you to stop coming."

Liall felt like he was two people: one standing and watching the terrible scene playing out in front of him, the other acting it out, his lips moving with the words, his strong hands reaching to tuck the blanket more warmly around the wasted, frail body.

"I know you did," he answered gently. "I can't help myself."

"Go away," the elderly Scarlet demanded. He jerked the blanket from Liall's hands with spotted, claw-like fingers. "I don't want to see you."

"But, love…"

"I'm not your love. I'm an old man who's no fit lover for anyone, nor any use either. Go away, Liall. Go back to your wife and children."

Liall's throat ached. "It's you I love. I've always loved you. No one else." He reached for Scarlet.

"Damn you!" the blasted body in the chair shrieked.

Scarlet's voice broke and he coughed pitifully, his voice a strangled whine. "*Leave!* I hate you! For Deva's sake, forget me and let me die in peace. Leave… never come back… *never, ever come back…*"

The wind howled in Liall's ears and clouds raced in front of his vision, whiting out everything. It took him long moments to realize the howling was his own. He was keening for what he'd done, for how he'd begged the curaes to treat Scarlet with every known remedy, with how he'd allowed them to extend Scarlet's life far past his natural time. But there was only so much the curaes could do.

Was this how it would end? Would he be a king still young compared to Scarlet, still virile and strong with many decades ahead of him, while Scarlet faded to a ruined, bitter frame of flesh that hated him, *hated him…*

"Please," Liall begged. "No." He covered his face and sank to his knees in the swirling void, bereft and alone.

Ulan took his arm.

"*Returnnnn,*" the Ancient breathed like a long moan.

The Hilurin room vanished. Liall took his hands from his face. The dagger was on the floor where he had dropped it. His eyes ached as if he had been weeping, and his nails had cut bloody half-moons into the palms of his hands, but he was not at the Blackmoat.

He was on his knees, looking up at Ulan. *A king kneels to no one.* He rubbed his hands on his breeches and felt like screaming. "What did I see?" He could hear the pleading in his voice. "Was that the future?"

"One future. Not the only one." Ulan bent his stiff body

and knelt until his eyes were level with Liall's. "Ressanda has secretly departed his barony. He sends his minion Hallin to distract you, to enrage you and keep you blind to his true purpose. Ressanda underestimates you. And me, for that matter." A *tock-tock* sound came from Ulan's chest; what might have been laughter. His eyes sparkled with lights deep within. "But a king has more eyes than his own, does he not? Even now, Ressanda journeys to Sul to play a game of soldiers and pawns with you, with his fair daughter as the queen."

Liall could not answer. Baron Ressanda. The army. The throne. What did anything matter if Scarlet died?

"I offer King Nazheradei a solution," Ulan said. "Scarlet does not have to die. He can have a life as long as any Rshani. Longer, if the legends prove true."

Liall shook his head, heartsick and afraid to believe. "That's impossible. You lie."

"Why should I lie? To lure you to Ged Fanorl? You are coming anyway. To bring Scarlet of Lysia there and capture him? There are much easier methods of taking one man, as Melev well knew. Even Melev did not *lie* to you. He chose a path and did not inform you. No Ancient has ever *lied.* Your t'aishka does not have to perish so quickly, so long before his time. The Shining Ones knew the path." Ulan stood up. "The answer waits in Ged Fanorl, in the hands of the King of Forever."

Later, Liall would realize that he caught at those words like a drowning man to a plank of wood. Time was his enemy now, so much so that he had begun to dislike waking and sleeping and every moment in between, except those hours when he could forget the future and lose himself in the scent of Scarlet's hair, in the feel of his skin pressed close. The tragedy he had just witnessed tore at him.

That must never happen, he swore silently. *It will never happen.*

Ulan offered him a lifeline and he clung to it with every fragment of his strength. He took the Ancient's hand and rose.

"Tell me," he commanded.

"You must travel the Temple Road to the Ironspell. Bring no Setna with you past the Blackmoat. Bring no weapons of iron past the Kingsdal."

The Temple Road. Cestimir had died on it, in the depths of a nameless ruin. "The Temple Road is hazardous," Liall said. "Between the Ironspell and the Kingsdal, the cold is a danger even to us. To Scarlet, it would be deadly. He won't make it."

"All shall be provided, in time," Ulan promised. He nodded slowly. "Nazheradei King must trust in me."

Oh, must I? Liall thought bitterly. "You mean for me to take a man of Hilurin blood into Ged Fanorl, under the mountain," he guessed. "At best, my people would see that as heresy. At worst, it would be treason. Every loyal subject of Rshan, even the ones who know Scarlet and love him, would turn on me. I would lose my crown, and then I'd lose my head."

"No."

"No, you say. Just *no* and I'm supposed to believe you."

"An Ancient does not lie."

The ache in his chest would not leave him. "What's in the mountain? Who is the King of Forever? Is it what Scarlet saw, the Creatrix?"

Ulan gave a hiss like steam. "So… Melev thought he could claim it. But did he desire it for Rshan, or for himself?"

Liall feared he had said too much. "It doesn't matter. Scarlet doesn't know where it is."

"The king lies."

He sighed, knowing it was hopeless. Ulan could tell truth from lies the way another man could tell black from white.

"You fear for nothing, Nazheradei. I do not desire the power of the Creatrix, and it rests in a place where none of my kindred can go: a mountain with an iron core."

"That much is true," Liall admitted. The Nerit. He had met Scarlet on Whetstone Pass, at the very top of Nerit Mountain. Was that an accident, like everything else? He was beginning to doubt that accidents existed. "But that doesn't stop you from sending others to claim it for you."

Ulan's mouth shriveled like a wizened apple into an expression of disgust. "The Norl Ūhn is deep and cold. Kalaslyn is brown and dry. At the end of that road is only death. We shall send no one to retake the Instrument of Making. No creature that thinks should ever have the knowledge of it. Let it be hidden in the dark until the mountains fall to dust."

There was such loathing in his voice that Liall dropped the subject. Ulan wasn't the least bit curious about the Creatrix. There were men in Rshan who would eviscerate Scarlet for the knowledge, if they had the slightest inkling he possessed it.

"As you wish," Liall said. "Scarlet will say nothing of it. He has given his oath."

"The vows of Anlyribeth can be broken," Ulan said cryptically. The lines of his face relaxed. "But not, I think, the word of Scarlet of Lysia." He swept his hand toward Liall's desk. "Bring to me your maps. I will show you the path."

Liall swallowed. "And what lies at the end of *that* road?"

"Life." Ulan bent until his eyes were on a level with Liall's. Opal sparks floated in the depths of his moonlike eyes, a sea of darting stars. "Life."

Bread and Roses

Scarlet hurried from the bedroom, half his virca unlaced, cursing a button that had decided to pop off as he was struggling to close the door. And the door was too gods-be-damned big, of course. It was like trying to close the gate to a stable.

He had grown so accustomed to boredom and dawdling in the mornings that when Liall sent a message to join him for breakfast, Scarlet went into a rush and promptly forgot where the servants kept everything. He could have called for Nenos to help him dress—Liall would certainly have approved of that—but the day he couldn't dress himself would be the day he'd hang up his pedlar's coat for good.

Like it isn't already hung, he thought with a sigh. He was no more a pedlar now than a rabbit was an antelope.

Liall was usually gone before he woke, and they had not had a morning meal together in weeks. Scarlet arrived with his virca still unlaced up the side. The dining room was warm and smelled wonderfully of bacon and apples, and he rushed in with an apology on his lips, only to find Liall was not there.

Tesk stood by the table, his hands folded behind his back. He smiled happily and bowed. "Ser," he greeted.

Scarlet glanced around, but other than the servants, they were alone. "Oh! Hello," he said, holding the laces of his virca together awkwardly.

Tesk came forward, his hands outstretched. "If you'll

allow me?"

"I suppose…"

Tesk began to lace the side of the virca with quick, practiced hands. "Do you not have your own manservant, ser Keriss?"

Scarlet shook his head. "I don't want one."

"May I ask why?"

"Because I learned to dress myself when I was three." Tesk's cologne smelled of jasmine and spice. When he bent to tighten the lower laces, Scarlet was very aware of Tesk's long, scented hair brushing his cheek. He wondered if Tesk was flirting with him. Surely not.

Scarlet cleared his throat. "But maybe not into one of these damned things."

"Precisely my point, ser. You either need a proper valet or a simpler mode of dress."

He'd already tried to return to Byzan clothing. It was just one more thing to make him stand out, to mark him as different. He'd made a promise to Liall to try to fit in and learn Rshani ways. Going back to tunics and pedlar's coats was a step backward, not forward. "I know," he said reluctantly. He raised his arm to let Tesk finish. "Maybe you're right."

Tesk knotted the last lace. "Of course I am. There." He straightened Scarlet's collar and stepped back. "Nicely done, if I do say so myself. If my art did not keep me so engrossed, I would apply for the position myself. There's an art to bathing a man, too, you know."

Scarlet felt his cheeks turning hot. "I don't believe Liall would approve."

Tesk arched a brow. "You think not?"

They both laughed at the same time.

"You're a terrible flirt, friend." Scarlet nodded at the table. "Sit and eat. Are we waiting for the king?"

Tesk waited for him to take a seat first, then eased into a chair across from him. The head of the table they left for Liall. "We are, but King Nazheradei asks that we begin without him. He was called away and will return shortly." He signaled to Chos to pour the che.

Scarlet murmured his thanks to Chos, the youngest of the servants. Chos gave him a dry smile in return, all eyes for Tesk. In the beginning, Chos had only been the bath attendant, which was an easy task and something one could do with little training. It was only recently that Nenos had moved Chos to full duties in other areas of their apartments, and replaced the bath attendant with a much older man who was very skilled. Privately, Scarlet was glad of it, since Liall was nearly obsessive about bathing, and that meant that Chos saw the king naked almost as much as he did. Chos had an avid eye. Scarlet decided he didn't care for that much.

"Is that rose che?" Tesk asked Chos sharply.

Chos froze in the act of pouring. "Yes, my lord."

Tesk waved his hand. "Take it away. This is not a morning for weak che. Dvi," he snapped his fingers for the cook. "Bring the northern black."

Dvi moved at once to obey.

"But my lord," Chos began.

Tesk turned a stare on Chos that made him swallow whatever he was going to say.

That look would freeze tree sap, Scarlet thought. He'd never seen Tesk so dangerously cold, or Chos so intimidated.

Chos collected the che cups and retreated quickly to the sideboard. Scarlet leaned forward. "What's amiss?" he whispered.

Tesk shook his head very slightly, barely moving his chin. "Try the eggs, ser. Dvi is a wizard with egg pie."

Puzzled, Scarlet helped himself and chewed while watching the doorway for Liall. Tesk did not speak until Dvi returned with the black che.

"I never did care for roses overmuch," Tesk sniffed.

Scarlet's thoughts again went to Ressilka. Jarad Hallin had named her the Rose Lady of Tebet. He wondered if Tesk was trying to be kind.

"The leaves of rose che must be young and weak if one is to taste the flower," Tesk went on. "But then that's all you taste." He sipped his che delicately. "I find the scent of roses rather insipid, myself."

Scarlet gave him a questioning look. Again, Tesk shook his head almost imperceptibly. Scarlet busied himself with his plate as he tried to puzzle it out. Things certainly were odd this morning.

The door opened and Liall came in like a storm, swearing a blue streak in Sinha and throwing his cloak at poor Dvi.

Scarlet caught some of the words, mostly to do with parentage and genitals and manure. His ears turned warm and he knew he must be blushing.

Liall looked at him and the flow of obscenities stopped. "Your pardon, Scarlet. I just had to deal with those…" There apparently wasn't a word for it in Bizye. Liall switched back to cursing in Sinha.

Tesk rose from his chair and bowed slightly. "Sire."

Liall didn't seem at all surprised to see Tesk. The king nodded and glanced around the room, empty but for servants and the three of them. "All is well?"

"Nothing out of place, my lord," Tesk said.

Scarlet pushed his plate away and reached for his che cup. "Deva save us, I'm afraid to ask. Is there some reason I can't drink the che I want in the morning?"

"It's nothing you need worry about," Liall said.

Tesk raised his chin. "I think he should be told."

"Of course you do," Liall answered in a flat voice. He looked at the servants. "That will be all."

Dvi bowed and turned at once to leave, but Chos lingered, che pot in hand. "Sire?"

"We'd like to be alone."

Chos's face turned pinched, and Scarlet felt a little sorry for him, but only a little. Chos bowed and left the room with his back stiff. A flustered and embarrassed Dvi followed.

"You've insulted him," Scarlet said. *Tell me what?*

Liall plucked the cup out of Scarlet's hand and took a

drink. He licked his lips. "He could use some insult," he muttered. "The lad is too full of himself."

"That sounds familiar."

"He's not you," Liall said, sour and adamant. "Not even close."

"Because he carries a wine jug to your table rather than goods between villages?" It wasn't like Liall to be so snobbish. Scarlet felt a rush of sympathy for Chos. Like him, Scarlet had been born a peasant, too. There were some who would never let him forget it.

"Because he makes sure I *know* he's carrying the wine jug," Liall answered. He put the cup down. "I don't want to discuss the damned servants."

"Then tell me what's happened." At Liall's look, Scarlet snorted. "You're not moving from this room until you do."

Liall's white brows went up and his expression lightened to amusement. "Is that so?" He shook his head. "As you will. You won't like it, I promise you. One of the horses died."

"Was killed," Tesk interjected.

"We don't know that for certain," Liall countered.

Scarlet's stomach lurched. "A horse." He paused. "One of the white ones?" Quieter: "One of hers?"

Liall nodded. "They'd had a hard crossing, and had to sail around the islands of Sul-na. The water is different here, as well as the feed. Animals are sensitive to such things."

"Not so sensitive that they drop dead from clean water and grain," said Tesk. "Theor inspected those horses just yesterday. He swears they were well."

"Why do you believe someone killed it?" Scarlet wished now he hadn't eaten. "What kind of point does it make to slay an innocent beast?"

Tesk glanced at the king.

"Well, don't stop now," Liall said. "Not unless you want to be imprisoned in this dining room with me. Tell him what you suspect."

Tesk gave Scarlet a kind look, as if asking forgiveness. "You know that we in the Nauhinir are very fond of you, ser Keriss. None of *our* people believe this, but Jarad Hallin has accused you of poisoning Lady Ressilka's bride gift."

Scarlet made himself take a slow breath before responding. "One, they're not bride gifts because she ent a bride. Not yet, anyway. Two, I don't have the best aim in the land, but be sure if I meant to harm Ressilka, I wouldn't miss her by a mile and hit a poor fucking horse in her place."

Liall laughed.

Tesk smiled and diplomatically lowered his eyes. "That it's a lie isn't the point. Someone dispatched that animal knowing you might be blamed. That makes it a plot."

If there was one plot, there may be more. "This palace is more stuffed with plots than a cat in a fish market. Is that what this is about?" Scarlet asked Tesk. "You sending my che back and acting so queer and all. Some idiot threatened to poison me because a horse died?"

"Not in so many words," Tesk admitted. "But rose che to avenge an insult to a Rose Lady? It would have been… precious. Just the kind of clumsy poetry I'd expect an imbecile of Hallin's stripe to send a message with."

"That bastard needs to get out my palace," Liall growled, humor gone, "before Tebet is short of a drover."

Scarlet had only just begun to think of the palace as his home, and the guards and courtiers as his friends, or at the very least not his enemies. He put his elbows on the table and cradled his forehead. "Gods."

Liall took his hand. "Put this from your mind. It was nothing—"

"It's not nothing!"

"No, of course not," Liall rushed to say. "I only meant to say there was nothing you could have done any differently."

"I could have walked away when Nevoi told me to," Scarlet said glumly. "But I stood there and argued with that purple-coated fool in front of his people. I gave him exactly what he wanted."

"I know it's your way to accept the weight of every problem on your own shoulders, but this is neither your doing nor your burden."

"It does feel very neatly planned, sire," Tesk put in. "Hallin doesn't know ser Keriss well enough to predict how he would react, but his spies may."

Liall fell silent, and Scarlet could tell he was thinking. Deciding.

"Don't do anything," Scarlet said. "Please, just don't."

"I agree," Tesk said. "As ser Keriss pointed out, we've already played his public game once."

"So now we play a private one." Liall nodded. "Very well. No response. Dignified silence. The court already chafes at a pack of commoners swaggering the halls like lords. Accusations and ill-behavior will make the Tebeti even less welcome."

"I think I can help that along." Tesk smiled. "There are so few occasions for palace gossip to serve the crown. I can't afford to miss the opportunity."

Scarlet sighed wearily. "Listen to the pair of you. Games and gossip. I'm tired of grown men acting like children. You don't need swords, you need a spanking."

Liall ruffled Scarlet's hair. "Just try it."

"There is one bit of pleasantness," Tesk said. He went to the sideboard and took up a folded cloth. He unrolled the cloth with a flourish, revealing a gold-embroidered flower on a red background. "Your badge, Lord Wild," he said proudly. "The flame flower. I designed it myself."

"It's for me?" Scarlet stood and traced the embroidery with a finger. "It's beautiful." He smiled up at Tesk.

"So you approve?"

"Approve? It's brilliant. My sister Annaya would just about burst if she could see this. She'd love it."

"We should send her a silk banner," Liall suggested. "A gift from Lord Wild of Nau Karmun."

"A few coins would be more welcome," Scarlet replied. "Annaya would cut the silk up for hair ribbons and smallclothes."

Tesk smiled. He folded the cloth and tucked it into his sleeve. "She sounds like an eminently practical girl."

"A woman now," Scarlet mused. "I miss her ever so

much. Thank you, Tesk."

Tesk nodded. He seemed happy. "You're most welcome, ser. And now, since my design passes muster, I have packing to do."

"Packing?" Scarlet echoed in dismay. "Where are you going?" He'd come to rely on Tesk's company, to look forward to seeing him. Tesk wasn't as formal with him as Jochi, and he cared less for rules. Scarlet felt like he was losing all of his friends.

Liall exchanged a look with Tesk. "Sit," he said gently. "I'll explain."

Tesk bowed and took his leave.

Scarlet sat and propped his elbows on the table morosely. "You're sending him away because the hunt went bad."

"What, punishing him for saving your life? Hardly." Liall sat down. "The army… my army… is on the march."

Scarlet's head jerked up. "Good gods. We're at war?"

Liall smiled. "That's the first time you've said *we* when referring to Rshan."

"Like you said, this is home now. For better or worse. What's happened?"

"Nothing that wasn't going to happen anyway," Liall said easily.

Scarlet got the impression that Liall was deliberately making light of his news. He scowled. "None of that. Tell me all of it."

"I did help move matters along," Liall admitted. "You know what occurred last year in Magur?"

"I know some from Jochi. The rest is what everyone knows about rebels and burning towns."

Liall rubbed his chin thoughtfully. "I did not give those orders. I won't denounce them, but it's not what I would have done, either. Magur had long been a thorn in my mother's side. The rebels who had taken root there said that an old queen putting forth a mere boy as her heir was proof of the weakness of an aging dynasty. No few agreed with them."

"Your mother proved them wrong."

Liall nodded. "That she did. Before that, there were small skirmishes on the borders of Sul and Uzna, too. Nothing overt, but all the signs were there for trouble on the horizon. You remember I told you of the Tribeland campaigns of my youth, yes? Our enemy was the Ava Thule. They live in *gers* and ice caves and are always on the move, savage as beasts and twice as dangerous." He paused. "Vladei paid the Ava Thule to join the rebels in Magur."

Scarlet tried to picture the kind of people who could dwell in a land the Rshani deemed too harsh for survival. He could not. "Deva's hells," he murmured.

Liall nodded. "And it nearly worked. If Vladei had been victorious, their combined forces would have moved on to Uzna Minor. Eventually, they may have fought their way to the palace gates. Whatever else they might be, the Ava Thule are peerless fighters. There may still be ambitious men attempting to use them for their own aims."

"Do you know the names of these men?"

Liall shook his head. "Not with enough certainty to accuse. With three members of the royal family dead, there's been far too much change in the realm. Hopefully, this war will unite the baronies against a common enemy. Rumors have been heard of the barony of Tebet planning to defect and declare their own king." His smile was bitter. "That won't happen, though."

"Why not?"

"The Blackmoat," Liall answered simply. "The Blackmoat is in Kalas Nauhin. The baronies of Tebet, Jadizek, Hnir, and S'geth are in Fanorl Nauhin, far north and on the other side of the continent. The Blackmoat is far from here, but it is much closer to us than it is to Tebet. Those northern baronies would have no chance of controlling the Blackmoat so far from their home base, and whoever controls *it* rules the kingdom, north and south."

Scarlet recalled the vision he had in the deadfall, when he was sure he was in the Overworld. "What is it, exactly? What do they do there?"

Liall pointed to the furnace in the corner, dark and cold because Scarlet preferred the scent of wood fires. It was black and round with bright metal chasing and clawed iron feet, and a round pipe funneling into the wall for fumes.

"That," he said. "I don't mean they weld furnaces. They produce the fuel to burn in them. It's a very old art. The Ancients built the Blackmoat, but not on their own. They followed a king named Ramung."

Scarlet covered his shock with a grunt and poured more

che. "I thought he was called the Red King?"

Liall looked at him sharply. "So he was. Jochi is a good teacher."

Scarlet bit back the comment: *Probably shouldn't have sacked him, then.* "Well, what happened to this King Ramung?"

"No one knows. He vanished in a blizzard years later, after a great disgrace that left many dead. There are shrines to him on the Temple Road. Without him, we might have all perished long ago, buried under ice in a land of ghosts."

"Was he a true king?"

"He was a Camira." Liall drained his che cup and stood. "But they also say the Camira could fly."

Scarlet snorted. He reclined in his chair as Liall summoned Dvi for his cloak. His mind churned with questions. The Blackmoat? Why did he hear of that place so much of late? Why was Liall so surprised that he knew about the Red King, and why was he dreaming of him?

If it was a dream. Was Scaja real? I thought so at the time.

"Is suspicion alone enough reason to go to war?" he asked.

"It's not the only reason," Liall assured him. "I'll tell you more about it on the road. I promise."

Scarlet blinked. "You're letting me come with you?"

Liall wagged a finger. "You were about to insist on coming. Don't deny it."

"I wasn't going to. One less argument sounds good to me."

Chos brought the cloak in Dvi's place. Liall sighed and took the cloak from Chos's hands when the servant tried to drape it on his shoulders. He fastened his brooch and fixed Scarlet with a measuring look. "Don't you want to know what dangers you face beforehand?"

Scarlet shrugged. He took a roll from the plate. "You've already said. They sound like Bledlanders to me, and I understand *them* well enough, all right."

"They're much worse than Bledlanders."

"If that's so, why haven't you wiped them out by now?"

Liall's brows went up. "Is that your counsel: kill them all?"

Scarlet bit into the roll, enjoying the rich flavor and soft texture that were nothing like the rough bread of Lysia. Only in a noble house in Byzantur would he have found such. A baker needs fine flour for good bread, and there had been none of that in his village, thanks to raiders like the Bled.

"Never had much pity for outlaws," he said, chewing. "Since my parents were murdered, even that is gone. As Scaja used to say: Pity one rat in winter, you'll have a litter by spring."

Liall made a humming sound. "I agree with your father's pragmatism, but these vermin are particularly difficult to exterminate. If you think the land is harsh and unforgiving here, you have not seen the glaciers of the north. A man can die in minutes if he loses his way, and there are predators up there that make snow bears seem like puppies. We never killed all the Ava Thule because we couldn't *find* them all. If pursued, they flee beyond even the borders of their own lands, beyond the Greatrift and into Whitehell, where no sane man or beast would follow. In the war, Jarek turned us back at the Greatrift. She didn't want to, but the Ancients asked her to show mercy. If she had not, it's likely that most of us would have died, too."

"The Ava Thule survived," Scarlet pointed out. "Some of them, at least."

"Yes, or a pack of them may have fled south, where we passed them by unknowingly. Just *how* they did it is not terribly important."

Scarlet rummaged in a painted bowl for an apple. Privately, he disagreed. If the Ava Thule survived one army, they could certainly survive another. "In Ankar, they tell tales of how men once lived in caves, without the knowledge of iron or fire."

Liall seemed interested. "What's your point?"

"All life just wants to *be*, Liall. Even when it shouldn't be able to, even when a thousand things are trying to kill it. Look at rabbits. There isn't a single animal in the wilds here that doesn't hunt them for food, and yet they thrive. If it's true for rabbits, how much more true is it for men?"

Liall's gaze was steady. "Maybe I should give you a seat on my council."

"Don't you dare."

Liall smiled grimly and glanced at the door.

Scarlet touched Liall's hand. "Stay a moment? I need to ask you something." He looked at Chos. Poor lad, he spent more time being dismissed than working. Chos bowed and left.

Liall brushed his fingers over Scarlet's cheek. "Ask away."

Scarlet bit his lower lip. "Can't you give Jochi back his post? He truly wasn't to blame for the hunt."

Liall sighed. "I admit, I was wrong to be so angry. He's not a soldier. I had unrealistic expectations of him. The man I put in his place will not have such difficulty."

And what man will that be? "Are you sacking him proper, then?"

"Am I what?"

"Making him leave the court?"

"Oh… no. He's asked to return to the Blackmoat and I've agreed. Now, eat well and look for me in the Leaf Court when you're finished. I want to ride out and see my lands before we leave tomorrow."

As soon as that? Scarlet fought down a feeling of unease. "How will we travel?"

"At first by sleigh, then horseback. Sul isn't terribly far, alas, so the comfort will be short-lived."

"I remember," Scarlet said. He had a sudden memory of the first night they had arrived at the Nauhinir; stepping out of the sleigh before the glittering nobles in the courtyard, how the diamonds in the queen's crown had blazed, how Shikhoza's eyes had been like chips of ice. There had been so much guarded violence in their faces, so much dislike and distrust. Things had changed in the Nauhinir since then. He felt welcomed here, even liked. He doubted matters would be the same on the road.

That misgiving must have shown on his face. Liall bent and kissed his forehead. "They may stare and talk, my beautiful t'aishka, but *all* of my people will come to love you one day. It's impossible not to."

"Pretty words." Scarlet smiled. "What should I expect in Sul?"

"You should expect to be treated like what you are. You're part of my family, part of *me*. In Rshan, being acknowledged as t'aishka is like being born to my name. You're a Camira-Druz now. Do you understand? Don't fret."

Scarlet remembered the vicious actions of the rough mariners on the *Ostre Sul*, and the Nauhinir was full of nobles and courtiers and those trained to behave better than their common brethren. He suspected that being in Sul openly as the king's t'aishka would be a great deal different than a day in the palace.

Whatever he felt, he wasn't about to let Liall see him hesitate to go journeying. He was a pedlar after all. *Besides, Liall's guards will be with us, and Deva knows how many thousands of soldiers. What could happen?*

He summoned a firm smile. "I'm not fretting, you want-wit. Off with you so I can stuff myself with more of Dvi's bread. There's precious few master bakers in your army, I'll wager."

"What are you doing?"

The voice was harsh, the tone unfamiliar. Scarlet jumped and turned, feeling guilty without knowing why. He had sought out Cestimir's rooms on instinct, not knowing if Liall had given them to someone else yet, some noble or Setna.

He'd found the wing empty, the door closed but not bolted. When he entered, the room was as fresh as if it had been cleaned yesterday.

A stern man stood in the doorway that led back into the hall. He was gray-eyed and had a strange streak of dark silver hair against the white at his temples.

"I'm—" Scarlet licked his lips. "I'm sorry. I don't know what I was looking for. I just wanted to come here before… before." He wished to see Cestimir's room one last time before they left the Nauhinir, but he didn't want to say that.

The man stepped into the room with him, peering left and right. "You should not wander so deep into the palace alone, ser."

"And who are you?"

"Margun." He closed the door.

Scarlet studied him. The words were cultured, but Margun was no courtier. His dress was too severe: a black virca with no ornament, riding boots that had seen heavy use, and worn leather breeches. His features were sharp, severe as a blade, and his face was scarred.

Not the kind of man to fool about with, Scaja would have said. Scarlet had no sense of danger, but Margun had a manner that reminded him slightly of Cadan. Or at least, Cadan as the man Scarlet had initially believed him to be, before the mask was torn away. A soldier?

He decided he didn't like the man. "Margun," he echoed. "Are you the master of my coming and goings, then?"

The gruff, commanding air vanished from Margun. He bowed his head. "No, ser. Not at all. If it please you, the king will be looking for you in the Leaf Court."

Scarlet frowned. "You seem to know my business rather well, and I haven't even heard your name before."

"Nor would you, my lord. I've only recently arrived at the palace."

I'm not a lord, rose to his lips. But Liall had given him the hunting lands, and presented him with some fancy paper that made him Lord Wild. *Like putting a hat on a mule,* he thought. *I'm no more a lord than this Margun is a cherry tree.*

"Why are you following me, Margun?"

"I am in the king's employ, ser. I saw you unattended, and this wing is unused since the prince's death. I thought perhaps I could help you."

The words were courteous and Margun kept his distance. Scarlet relaxed. "Oh," he said. He glanced around the room. It had a narrow bed and a reading table. The walls were gray stone with touches of blue. Plain wool curtains. Iron shields on the walls. It was a somber and depressing room for a boy as young as Cestimir. The only colors were the spines of books in a tall iron case.

Scarlet ran a finger over the brilliant leather covers. "Did you know Cestimir?"

"I did not, ser. He was quite young and I haven't visited the Nauhinir in… some time."

Scarlet smiled bitterly as he pulled a book with a crimson spine from the case. Was that what Liall meant when he spoke about tact? More to the point, about how Hilurin didn't have any. "He was three summers younger than me. What you meant was he wasn't even born the last time you were here. You're Liall's age, I suppose."

"I'm much older than the king, I believe."

He sighed. Margun looked to be in his prime, no more than forty years, as the Aralyrin counted them. Certainly younger than Scaja. "Of course you are. Your lot live forever."

Margun smiled. It didn't suit his face. "I wish that were true, ser."

Scarlet opened the book and tried to read the first page. The only words he could recognize were *mountain* and *forever*. And one other: a rune distinctly out of place among the elegant Sinha script, scrawled large over an entire corner of the page. He turned the page quickly to cover his shock. "So, how old are you, then?"

Margun tilted his head. A scrawl of hair the color of lead slipped over his shoulder. "Are you always so impolite?"

Scarlet raised his eyebrows. "That's plain speech, right enough. Now I really believe you're new to the palace." He flipped the pages. "And no, I'm not. Or, well… I try not to be. It's hard to know what offends one of you giants."

"I see," Margun answered coldly.

"For Deva's sake, what did I say now?"

"Other than refer to me as a creature instead of a man, not a thing."

Scarlet sighed and snapped the book shut, knowing he was in the wrong and nettled by it. "I apologize. Now will you please go and let me say goodbye to Cestimir in peace?"

Margun swept his hand at the empty apartments. "Ser, the prince rests at the Kingsdal. Do you think he can hear you from here?"

Scarlet tucked the book under his arm. "Yes. I do." He folded his hands and waited.

After a long moment, Margun bowed and opened the door. "I will be within hearing, ser. At least until you rejoin the king."

With Margun gone, Scarlet walked slowly through the still and empty rooms, his heels echoing on the floors with a lonely sound. He went deeper into the center of the wing, where there were no candles lit and no windows, only darkness all around. To his eyes, every edge in the room was silver, the contours of the walls and the shapes of objects illuminated in relief, as if splashed by stark moonlight.

Cestimir had few personal effects in sight: a stuffed white bear tucked in a glass case, a little flute made of bone, and—above the cold fireplace—a tall painting of a woman with a strawberry shine to her pale gold hair.

Scarlet looked up at her. Ressilka's mouth was curved in a beguiling smile, her large eyes lined with blue paint, and her arms full of roses. Dew sparkled on the rose petals and dampened the breast of her pink gown, and her amber neck was clasped by a necklace like a spider web dripping with precious blue sapphires.

He recognized it. He should, since it belonged to him

now. The necklace was an heirloom of Queen Nadiushka's family. It was supposed to be Shikhoza's bride gift, but her wedding day never came and the queen gave it to Scarlet before she died.

How Ressilka came to be wearing it for the portrait, he didn't know. He found he didn't care to know, either.

"You can't have him," he whispered to her image. He turned away from her to address the room. "I'm sorry, Cestimir," he said, watching a little spider spin a silver thread from the mantel to the floor. "So sorry I don't even have the words, but not sorry enough to stop loving Liall, or to step aside and let her take him from me. I know you loved her. I'll look after her for you. I promise."

He retreated through the lonely rooms and paused at the main door. "And thanks for the book."

He closed the heavy door after him with the same unmistakable feeling that he had when he prayed to Deva, the deep instinct that he had been *heard*.

The rune he recognized in the book was one of the few known well by Hilurin. He had seen it painted on the crossroads of the Old Salt Road between Rusa and Lysia as a dire warning to travelers, and he had seen it in his vision of the Overworld.

The rune was *Senkhara*, the god of the Minh.

Liall was not in the Leaf Court when Scarlet came down.

The portcullis—a giant iron affair, forged in a pattern of thorny vines and leaves—was open. Fires were blazing in great iron pits throughout the yard, driving out the lingering chill.

The courtyard alone was bigger than the whole village square of Lysia, surrounded by walls twenty feet high and three feet thick, overshadowed by the towering structure of the massive palace itself, which rose like a pale mountain topped with spires and towers and endless stairs. The Leaf Court was one of many such yards in the Nauhinir. Scarlet had never bothered to count them all.

He spotted Theor by the gatehouse. The master of horse wore leather armor over a padded gambeson and was saddling a blue-black horse of alarming size.

The horse dipped his neck low and snuffled when Scarlet came near. He held out his hand to let him sniff. "Hello, boy. Big fellow, ent you?"

Theor watched. "The beasts like you." One broad hand the size of a plate gentled the horse's mane.

"He just wants a treat," Scarlet said, but he was pleased.

Theor shook his head. "I've been watching them. When you come into the stables, it's as if a summer wind blows through the pens. They look for you."

Scarlet smiled and ducked his head. "My father was a wainwright. I'm just comfortable around horses. Maybe they sense that."

"No," Theor said. His gaze was level, measuring him. "They sense a kind spirit, and maybe that you have a weakness for them. You never visit your pony without a treat."

Scarlet chuckled at Theor naming his mount a pony. That animal was as big as any horse in Byzantur. "Where is Apples? I thought I'd be riding him today?"

Theor turned and searched the yard. "I did order him to be saddled, ser. Damn that fool groom. Serves me right for letting a green boy do my work. If you will hold Argent, I'll bring him."

Scarlet took the reins, surprised that Theor trusted him to control the horse. "Yes, of course," he murmured, looking up at the great black head. If Argent bolted, he'd be dragged like the tail on a kite.

Argent snuffled his hair, seeming as amused as a horse could be.

Scarlet stroked the silken lines of Argent's neck and clucked his tongue soothingly as Theor strode off.

The guards changed duty at the gatehouse as he waited, and servants came and went through side doors into palace kitchens and up winding stairs that led high into open battlements and parapet walks. Black smoke curled up in twisting ropes from the fires and vanished over the walls. Scarlet stamped his feet and wiggled his toes in his boots. The sun might be warmer on his shoulders today, but the ground was cold as ice. Liall said only the top layers of the land would melt. Deeper below, it had remained frozen for thousands of years.

Two columns of freeriders came in through the open gates, leather-clad and grim as winter, their long white hair flying in the wind. Their horses were as weathered as the riders. Grooms scurried to bring the men water and their mounts grain, for by law, the freeriders who patrolled the roads and highways in the king's service were entitled to shelter anywhere, even the palace.

Theor returned with a face like a thundercloud. Liall followed him, blue cloak whipping around his knees, his shoulders hunched.

Whatever was wrong, Argent seemed to feel it, too. The beast turned his head to watch Liall and exhaled heavily from the great bellows of his lungs.

"We're leaving for Sul now," Liall said without preamble. His fists were clenched.

"Where's my horse?" Scarlet asked Theor.

"Now," Liall said, his jaw tight. He took the reins from Scarlet's hands. "Theor, return Argent to the stables. Call for me when the sleigh is ready."

"Yes, my Lord." Theor patted Argent's neck, who had sensed the change and begun to chew the bit.

Scarlet waited until the master of horse was out of earshot. He looked at Liall. "Is it bad?"

Anger flashed over Liall's features. "I'm sorry, Scarlet. Apples can't make the trip to Sul."

"Is he ill?" At Liall's nod, Scarlet turned to follow Theor. "Let's go to him. I could cast a withy. Magic works on animals, too, you know."

Liall took his arm and drew him back. "I think you shouldn't."

Scarlet stared, trying to puzzle out why Liall wouldn't

want him in the stables. Then, he knew. "That prancing purple bastard," he swore. "Did he hurt the poor creature just to stick a pin in me? I'll stick one in him!"

I'll set his boots on fire, he thought darkly. *I'll make him burn like the sails of the Minh ship.*

Liall grabbed his shoulders. "Scarlet, stop!"

Only then did he realize that his hands were burning with heat. He smelled smoke and tore his gloves off, throwing them on the ground.

Liall seized his hands and examined them. "Are you hurt? Are you burned? T'aishka, *look at me.*"

Scarlet shook his head, trying to clear the fiery haze from his mind. "I'm fine. I just… fine. I'm sorry." He took a deep breath and stared at his hands in amazement.

Liall's fingers were trembling. "Gods below, what was that?"

What, indeed? Was he really thinking of setting Jarad Hallin on fire in the stables, around all that hay and timber? It would have gone up like a torch, along with the horses.

"I was imagining Hallin hurting Apples. And then it got away from me." He looked at his palms. They were flushed pink. "It's becoming hard to control," he whispered in a shaking voice. "When we left Byzantur, I could barely summon a withy big enough to light a candle. Now…" He shivered, suddenly cold. "Now there's a lion chained under my skin. It wants to devour everything. I try to starve it by not using magic, but it only grows hungrier."

Liall's blue eyes were wide. "Can it harm you?"

Scarlet frowned. *Could it?* He exhaled, growing calmer. No one was hurt. It hadn't gotten away from him this time. "I don't think so. My dad always said that Deva's gift to us was drawing the magic out, that it had been inside of us from the beginning. Can one flame harm another?"

"A greater flame can overpower a smaller one, yes. The small flame is absorbed, the larger prevails." Liall rubbed his thumb over Scarlet's palm. "But we won't play philosophy with your life. We must find a way to master this magic of yours."

Scarlet nodded helplessly. They must, but how? He had no one to turn to in this. No father, no mother, no village. In Lysia, he could have asked old Hipola, or Jerivet, who was a wonder with animals. "Is Apples going to be alright?"

"He'll live," Liall said. "Theor will make sure of that."

"I want to help."

Liall shook his head. "No more dancing to Hallin's tune. I wouldn't wager money on his survival if either one of us confronted him right now. Let's leave him here to shovel the shit from his damned *bride gift*."

Scarlet spied Alexyin approaching from the stable gates. He knew they weren't going anywhere until Alexyin had his say.

"Sire," Alexyin greeted Liall with a respectful nod, and a shorter one in Scarlet's direction, which was better than no acknowledgement at all. Scarlet suspected the dry courtesy was for Liall's benefit. Alexyin saw the burned gloves on the ground and shot a curious look to Liall.

Liall ignored that look and glanced at the stable gates.

"Theor told you?"

Alexyin nodded. "He did. I should speak with the Tebeti, allay any fears the delegation might have regarding the incident, if there are any."

"You've got to be joking," Scarlet blurted.

Liall took his hand. "Hush," he said, not unkindly. He glared at Alexyin. "That's your advice? Appeasement?"

"It's a horse, sire," Alexyin said flatly.

"It's a message!" Liall shot back. "And a threat. I had to send Tesk to guard my apartments—*my* apartments in *my* home—because of this."

"The very last thing they want is for you to come to harm."

"Well, of course," Liall mocked. "Without me, there's no royal wedding, is there? Don't play the mummer. You know what I fear."

"A fear we all share, sire," Alexyin said easily.

Too easily.

Liall's eyes narrowed. He dropped Scarlet's hand and stepped close to Alexyin, nose-to-nose. "Do we?" he asked softly.

Scarlett heard the red violence in Liall's voice and shivered.

Alexyin met Liall's gaze calmly. "I am loyal, my lord."

"If I believed otherwise, I'd be having this conversation with a head impaled on a spike; one that was lately a Setna."

Alexyin's jaw dropped. "Nazheradei … my Prince…"

"Your king," Liall reminded him.

Alexyin was shaken and seemed to grope for words. "Sire, I am sworn to the Camira-Druz. Sworn for life. I'm only a man, but I'm faithful and I advise the crown to the best of my ability." He squared his shoulders. "Wars are perilous and uncertain. Before the first battle begins, my earnest counsel is for you to marry Lady Ressilka. At once." His glance shifted to Scarlet for an instant. "A king may keep a consort and still take a wife."

"Just one consort?" Liall bantered back. "Why stop there? Is that why you prompted the baron of Jadizek to offer me a formal mistress?"

"He what?" Scarlet roared. Heads turned all over the yard.

Alexyin ignored him. "My lord, this is how alliances are made," he said with patience. "How they have always been made, with marriage and children and beds."

Scarlet could keep quiet no longer. "D'you know the difference between a Rshani court and a brothel? The brothels post their prices on the front door!" he stormed. "Giant, piss-mucking, whoremongering, sons of—" his curses descended into gutter Falx.

A wry grin curled a corner of Liall's mouth. He made no move to stop the tirade, though Alexyin looked like he'd swallowed a fish whole and was choking on the fins.

"—pack of turd-smelling goat-fuckers!" Scarlet finished, breathing heavily.

Liall shrugged. "And there, my learned advisor, is your answer. No mistress, from Jadizek or anywhere."

Alexyin's nostrils flared. "Cestimir was a prince who

heeded his counselors!"

"Perhaps that's why he's *dead,"* Liall shot back.

Alexyin snapped his mouth closed in shock. He threw Scarlet a look of pure venom before bowing deeply to Liall. "As my king commands."

Scarlet was shaking as he watched Alexyin vanish into the palace. Liall took him in his arms and stroked his hair.

"We're leaving," Liall whispered into his ear. "You longed to go adventuring again, my redbird. I fear what's coming will be much more than you bargained for."

They took fifty men and sheltered at a freerider's fort a thousand feet below the Nauhinir. Scarlet could see the towers of the palace from his window, the points of spires glittering in the sun. He'd seen it from a distance before, but now that he was leaving, it was like looking back on a dream. He was shocked to realize that he considered the Nauhinir as home now. That impossibly immense palace—dwarfing the king's castle at Ankar—and filled with grand halls and wealth and strangeness; how could that ever be his *home?*

Because it's Liall's home, he thought.

He turned from the window and crawled into the bed. The ranger had given up his room to the king, and Liall had gone to take supper with his men. Scarlet had begged off, saying he was tired after the incident at the Leaf Court. Liall had nodded and offered to send for a curae, but Scarlet had refused. A quiet place to sleep was all he wanted.

A small fire smoldered in the hearth of the ranger's room, which was quite large for one man. Scaja's little cottage would have fitted entirely inside of it. He reclined against the deep pillows and closed his eyes, trying to picture his home: the painted window, his narrow bed in the back of the cottage, the weave of the woolen curtain that had separated it from the larger room. It was the only home he had ever known, before Liall. He couldn't see the cottage in his mind, but he could smell phantom smoke. He sighed and rolled over. It was futile to dwell on sadness.

What month must it be now? he wondered. Liall said it was Greentide in Rshan, so… the Month of Kings?

The trade routes from Rusa would be open, or would they? Had his entire country dissolved into civil war, as Liall had predicted, or had the Flower Prince found a way to make peace with the Aralyrin?

Rannon's caravan would have been on the move for months. He wondered how the old bastard was, if he'd found someone to make him happy or was still spending his evenings drinking himself blind and staring into campfires. He hoped the man was well.

I'd have been dead thrice over if he hadn't taught me the long-knives, he thought. Rannon was owed a prayer to Deva for that, at least. And for much else.

"*On danaee Deva shani,*" he whispered. He turned his head to look at the patch of sky. "Remember my family, Goddess. Bless the souls of my father and my mother, who wait for me in the Overworld. Please watch over Annaya and Shansi. They're going to need it, I think. Bless Rannon, even though he's a slaver and probably doesn't deserve it or even believe in you. He's got a hard heart, but he never went looking for that. The world gave it to him, poor man. Bless Liall, because he's a good king and wants to be a better one. Bless my friends Tesk, Jochi, Nenos, and Nevoi. Oh, and Alexyin, too. He doesn't like me much, but maybe that isn't his fault either. *On danaee Deva shani."*

His prayers said, he opened the book he had taken from Cestimir's room. It was a fine volume, the leather perfect and the binding flawless. He found the page he was looking for and put his thumb near the rune, careful not to touch it.

Senkhara. He squinted at the Sinha words on the page, understanding little. It was some kind of story about a place in the mountains. Or… no. He frowned. *Inside* a mountain. It might be the story Liall told him about the sacred mountain. He flipped the pages of fine script until he found another rune, and the floor dropped out from beneath the bed.

The air turned cold.

It took him a moment to realize he was outside, standing in the snow and darkness. *But it's spring,* he thought. The land was lit with a cold blue twilight that illuminated the distant contours of ice hills and black cliffs.

"I'm dreaming," he said, even though he knew he wasn't. Fear slammed into him.

"Here," called a voice behind him.

Scarlet whirled. The gray-eyed man had a face now. "The stranger," he whispered.

"The king," the man answered. A bloated moon rose swiftly over a hill behind him, throwing his face into shadow again.

The moon shimmered and changed to a giant wheel, turning slowly in the heavens as stars with long tails of cinders fell from the sky and the ground vibrated beneath his feet like a heartbeat.

Scarlet stood rooted to the spot, unable to move as the man approached with deliberate steps. The wind howled and the stranger's long red robes slapped wildly against his body, moving like a living thing.

The red king, he thought, shivering. "Stay away from me," he quavered. His hand dropped to his hip, but his long-knives weren't there. His world shrank to a single point of fear and dread. "Who are you?"

The stranger pressed his hand to Scarlet's cheek. "I am the King of Forever."

The touch burned with a heat like sun-warmed steel. A fire leapt through Scarlet's skin and seared along his nerves to his brain. One by one, the stars winked out. The wind stilled. Even the twilight dimmed, leaving him in a blank void containing nothing but him, the stranger, and the burning hand.

"Remember, blood of Lyr. Wake and return."

He woke in the bed with Liall snoring softly beside him, remembering only the fragment of a dream where he was cold and alone.

Forever

A light snow lashed at the blue windows of the opulent sleigh as it crossed the bridge to Sul. The Queen's Bridge was the only marker of the city boundaries that Scarlet claimed to recognize.

"I thought pedlars were excellent wayfarers," Liall teased. "Yet you can't remember the route between Sul and the palace."

Scarlet wore black velvet for this journey, and the fabric against his ivory skin made him seem more beautiful than possible, more like a dream than life. *I knew I could not be this lucky,* Liall thought. *There's always a price for happiness.*

"It was *dark*," Scarlet protested.

"You can see in the dark."

"Oh, hush."

When they reached the city proper, Scarlet nearly plastered himself to the window, staring wide-eyed at everything and asking a hundred questions.

"Why would you want to know where they store the fish, for Deva's sake?"

"Because I was wondering if they ever thaw out, and if you smoke them first or what happens to the stores of them when the weather warms up."

Liall chose to be amused. "I thought you'd be more engrossed with your history book." He tapped the cover of the thin volume Scarlet had taken from Cestimir's room. At first, Scarlet had been hesitant to say where he got it, and seemed relieved when Liall was pleased at the answer.

"He's dead, my love," Liall had said. "I had little time with my brother, but I think it would make him happy to know that you're reading his books."

The sleigh hissed over snow that was still thick enough on the roads to allow travel this way. A few more weeks and it would all be melted.

Scarlet shrugged. "Some of the pictures tell me what's happening, but I still can't read Sinha for shit."

Liall laughed. "You're still thinking like a pedlar. And cursing like a mariner lately, I might add. Have someone read it to you."

"Who?"

"Anyone who can speak Bizye. Have Tesk find someone. He'll be happy to appoint an interpreter for you."

"I'd rather have Jochi," Scarlet groused.

"We've spoken of this. Jochi's fate will take him on a different path."

"Then I can do it on my own."

Liall took the book from Scarlet's lap and opened to a random page. He pointed at a word. "What does that say?"

Scarlet looked out the window, his lower lip mutinous.

Liall sighed, even as he adored the look of that lip. "My sweet love, you must become accustomed to having authority over others. It's part of your life here. They will not respect you if you insist on being equal to everyone."

"I don't know that I want the kind of respect that folk give to generals and kings and such. Your lot might think it's respect, but it's mostly fear. You forget: I was one of those folk. They let you *think* they look up to you."

"I have no illusions that every respect paid to me is sincere," Liall said. "Nor am I a fool. I lived among common folk in Byzantur, too, lest *you* forget. I know very well what the average man thinks of the nobility." He turned thoughtful. "But when they need us, Scarlet, when famine comes, or plague or war, it's the nobles they look to for guidance. They may resent us, but most believe that the differences between our fortunes are ordained."

"Rshani don't believe in gods. You don't even believe in luck."

"There are gods and there is destiny," Liall said smoothly, not bothered a bit. "We do not pray to gods, but we have temples and shrines, and we have reverence for those things beyond our knowledge, respect for the worlds unknown to us. We also have ceremonies, as you saw when I brought back the sun."

Scarlet snorted at mention of the Greentide ritual. "You should have been a mummer, as well as you played that." He smoothed his hand over the leather binding of Cestimir's book. "Worlds unknown… you mean the Overworld? That sounds like worship to me. I think Rshani must have gods after all. You just have no names for them."

Liall noticed that Scarlet's breath was misting the air when he exhaled. "It's grown cold in here." He twitched the furs over Scarlet's legs and drew him closer, sighing at the sweet feel of Scarlet's body in his arms. *I will never get used to how familiar his shape is to me, how dear the curves of his face and the warmth of his skin. One moment it seems like I've loved him a thousand years, and the next like we just met.*

"I thought it would be warmer near the sea," Scarlet said. He curled the laces of Liall's shirt around his finger.

"Hm, no. The wind off the water makes it colder sometimes, though generally it is warmer in Sul by now. The far north stays frozen year round."

"It does? I didn't know that."

"Spring is slow to come this year. People are calling it an omen."

"And blaming me for it, no doubt, as well as every mare that throws her foal early and every cask of spoiled beer."

Liall did not answer. It was true, so there was nothing to be said.

"And what do you think it is?" Scarlet asked.

"I think it's nothing," Liall answered firmly. "The weather is often strange, not only here, but in every country and island of Nemerl. Once, I was traveling in Morturii and saw a tower of whirling red sand as high as the walls of Rusa. A strange heat swept across the Channel that year, carrying a sour stench and clouds of tiny black flies. Half the crops in Ankar withered from it. Was that an omen?"

Scarlet shrugged. "Perhaps. I don't remember a famine in Morturii, though. What year was that?"

It was long before Scarlet was born. "I don't recall."

"It's too bad the spring is late. I was looking forward to a little sun and heat." Scarlet shifted nearer to Liall's warmth, but the next moment he sat straight up. The first of the tall rigging lines in the harbor had come into view. "Oh look! The ships! Look at all the ships. *Oh,* how beautiful they are."

"You've seen the harbor before," Liall reminded fondly.

"I was scared out of my wits and hardly knew where I was," Scarlet scoffed, his nose nearly pressed to the glass. "I don't remember half of it. Oh look! What's that?"

Liall tried to see where Scarlet was pointing. "That? That's a *razka kul.* A sword of the sea. A warship."

Scarlet's voice was hushed in awe. "I've never seen anything so… so…"

Liall was pleased. "I'm not surprised you've never seen one. They don't sail to Kalaslyn, but far southwest to the island kingdoms of Artinia and the Serpent Sea." He looked with appreciation at the majesty and soaring lines of the warship, and at the forbidding row of cannon lining her sides. "To my knowledge, there are no ships in the world to equal them. They are the queens of the water. Even the heavy Artinian ships will flee from them."

"And what's that little thing beside her?"

Liall looked again. "A sloop."

Scarlet laughed. "Is it really? Why's it painted like a cloud?"

"For camouflage." The sloop was single-masted, fore-and-aft-rigged, with a short bowsprit and a single headsail. The sails were gray with splashes of white, the boat painted in gray colors as well to mingle with the frequent mists and snows of the Rshani coastline. "Do you see the large wooden creature attached to the bow? That's a water dragon. The sloop is a patroller; swift on the water and built for speed. It's done up like that to fool the dragons and keep it safe."

"Dragons," Scarlet snorted. "You teased me once about that. There's no such thing."

Liall leaned in to kiss his ear. "Just as there are no such things as magic or Shining Ones or the Land of Night. The creature that statue represents is not truly a dragon, but it's large, fast, and destructive, so they call it a dragon. I'm no mariner, so I'm not the one to argue the point with you."

"I thought you liked the sea."

"I do indeed, but that does not make me a mariner. I thought you hated the sea?"

"I do, but I like the ships." Scarlet chuckled softly. "Think how far a journeyman could go aboard one of those. You could get all the way to the end of the world."

Liall smiled. "We are at the end of the world, and we are a pair of contradictions. It suits us."

A knock came at the roof of the sleigh. Liall pushed the furs off. "Put your cloak on, and your new gloves."

Scarlet's cloak was charcoal gray with the badge of Camira-Druz stitched on his right shoulder and pinned with a platinum snowbear. The gloves were black with crimson cords, lined with the fur of a white fox.

He pulled them on slowly and held his hands up to admire their fit. The left glove was narrower than the right, custom-made to accommodate his missing fifth finger. Liall had ordered them from the glover weeks ago, and a good thing, too, considering what had happened to Scarlet's last pair.

"Thank you for these. I've never had gloves so fine all for my own." Scarlet tightened the cords on the left glove.

Such a small hand, Liall thought. It was hard to believe Scarlet could kill with it. If he hadn't seen it with his own eyes, he might not have believed it, either.

"Will we be able to see the ships while we're here?"

"Perhaps tomorrow, if I can get away. Tesk will take some guardsmen and escort you to the Bleakwatch while I meet with the barons." Liall brushed a quick kiss to his hair again. "This isn't a pleasure trip, t'aishka."

Scarlet smiled. "Never fear, I know very well what we're up to. Battles and war and blood, right? But I won't apologize for being selfish and wanting more of you to myself."

"Wanting me is a vice I can bear from you." The sleigh slowed and ground to a stop at the bottom of a high hill, and the door swung open. Liall climbed out and gave his hand to Scarlet.

Scarlet exited the sleigh and looked around. The cadre of armed soldiers greeting them were already down on one knee to Liall. Liall motioned for them to rise and greeted their captain with a curt nod.

Snow-capped mountains were at their backs. Southward, the land continued to slope steeply to the waterline and the sprawling, busy harbor. The streets were lined with shops, warehouses, and mills, all glowing with blue lamps.

The North Sea spread out into the horizon, gray as lead and shrouded in mist. Choppy swells of waves tipped with white foam and chunks of ice battered the sea wall with booming sounds like thunder.

Liall saw Margun at the head of a column of armed men in matching uniform adorned with splashes of red. Tesk dismounted and bowed.

"Escort ser Keriss to the Bleakwatch," Liall said. "See that he is comfortable and the tower secure." The soldiers were watching curiously as he bent to kiss Scarlet's mouth. "I will join you as soon as I can." He winked. "Be patient. There will be plenty of ships in the harbor tomorrow."

The men who had come to greet them were not Nauhinir palace guards, but soldiers from the ranks of the queen's army. *The king's army now,* Liall thought. They were Jarek's sworn men, but they were unknown to him.

"Come, ser," Tesk said, and Liall was glad of the artist's presence. Scarlet knew few others in their retinue besides Jochi and Alexyin, and there was a more brittle chill between Scarlet and his old mentor. That was his fault, he supposed.

I should not have said that about Cestimir, Liall thought regretfully. Well, it was done now. With time, he might be able to mend it, but he couldn't make a broken che cup like new again.

Scarlet gave Liall a farewell kiss before following Tesk to the waiting horses. Margun Rook abandoned his position at the head of his column to shadow Scarlet closely. That man knew his business at least.

Alexyin stood near the soldiers. He bowed as Liall approached.

"I'd forgotten how busy it was here," Liall said, striving for a casual tone. "I've been behind palace walls too long. It seems positively frantic."

"I'd hardly call this frantic," Alexyin scoffed. "Preoccupied, perhaps."

Liall cleared his throat. "Alexyin… about what I said—"

"Forgotten, my king. The heat of the moment. I should not have pressed you on the matter."

Alexyin met his gaze, and Liall saw with relief that it was true. He smiled. "I'm glad. I want us always to be friends, Alexyin."

"On that we fully agree. It's my dearest wish, sire."

Pleased, Liall clapped Alexyin on the shoulder and mounted the horse that a guard held for him. This guard was in black and silver with a starred badge on his cloak: queen's men of Starhold, the great fortress of Nau Karmun, sworn to Nadiushka. *My men now,* Liall thought, and wondered if he would ever stop thinking of his kingdom as something borrowed, rather than his by birthright.

Alexyin took charge of the soldiers and guards and commanded their rank to his liking, and when he seemed satisfied, he gestured and the column began to move. He then took his place beside Liall, in the center of the protective box of alert guards. Behind the mounted column, a short train of foot-soldiers took up the march. Every man had an excellent sword at his hip, and the mounted guards held steel-tipped pikes.

"Is the Bleakwatch secured?" Liall asked.

"Khatai Jarek made it so before she left, sire," Alexyin said. "Filled all the available rooms with your own guards and cleared the first floor."

Bleakwatch was the baronial tower of Sul, a heavily-armored structure that loomed high over the bay and was well away from Arrowgate, the city armory. "We will only be here for two days. Has she sent word?"

"She gave the orders here for the conscription before she moved to Starhold to oversee the soldiers returned from Magur. The troops from Uzna Minor should arrive there before you."

"Who did she leave in charge?"

"Her third: Kamaras."

Liall knew the woman, though it had been many years since they had met. "She's capable."

Alexyin looked left and right as they rode, and all around them the crowds stopped and gaped at the royal procession before bowing low. "I do not like all this traveling in the open, with only these few to keep you safe," he grumbled. "Most of them are guards, not true fighting men."

"You'd prefer soldiers?"

"I prefer blooded men to guard the throne. Prince Cestimir would not have it so, and I've lived to regret his decision."

It was the first time Liall had heard of Cestimir making such a choice. "He refused guardsmen?"

"He refused soldiers. He said the household guards were enough, because they *were* common. They were his people. He said that if a king could not walk safely among his subjects, then he had no business being king."

"Wise words," Liall murmured.

"Idealistic words. A king should heed his counselors and leave his fine principles for when he can afford them."

Liall wanted no further arguments and he would say nothing against Cestimir. It was far too late, in any case. Hindsight would change nothing.

Alexyin sighed heavily and changed the subject. "Your pardon, my lord. Old habits. I hope Jarek has no trouble gathering the conscription from Uzna Minor. We need those men badly."

"Shikhoza knows what the smart move is, and Jarek will do as she's been commanded. Woe betide the man or woman who stands between Jarek and her duty."

The king's company crested the hill of the cobbled avenue, and Liall looked out over the wide mouth of Swan Bay and the whipping sails of the ships. There were more than he could count at a single glance, nearly a hundred of them. He inhaled deeply of the salt air and thought back to the day when he had first left Rshan, and how he had been so certain he would never return. He'd had an escort that day as well, only they were sent to see that the queen's command was carried out and that her only living son was exiled from Rshan's shores.

In his mind, he could still see the grief on Jarek's face as she turned away from him, leaving him on the deck of a hulking merchant ship bound for Ankar.

"Nothing stops Jarek after she's been given her orders," he said quietly. "Nothing and no one."

The armory of Arrowgate had nothing to recommend it but weapons. Otherwise, it was a tower of stone on the lip of the harbor, two hundred feet high and facing the sea with sixty cannon pointed into the bay. Liall had frequented tabernas in Volkovoii that were better appointed. At least Arrowgate was cleaner.

The great hall was paneled with ancient planks. Massive vaulted beams overhead had been scavenged from shipwrecked vessels, with ancient barnacles still clinging to the wood as proof. The floor was slate flags, and several dusty kegs—long dry of wine—were upended and used as chairs around the moot table. They had managed to find one proper chair for the king: a throne made of oak and hammered bronze, probably taken from the captain's office.

Liall took his seat and left the kegs for Ressanda and his company. Arrowgate was one of the poorest halls that Sul had to offer, but Ressanda's poor behavior deserved no better greeting.

Baron Ressanda wasted no time getting to the point.

"I have come for the wedding of my daughter," he announced. Red-bearded, big-bellied, and loud, the baron was nevertheless a nobleman and he bellowed like one when he was crossed.

Liall tipped his wine cup to Ressanda in a toast. "Lovely. Who is she marrying?"

This red branch of my House needs to lower his voice before I forget myself and snap him like a twig, he thought. He recalled Ulan's warning: *Even now, Ressanda journeys to Sul to play a game of soldiers and pawns with you, with his fair daughter as the queen.*

Ressanda's face darkened at those words. "My king makes a joke of me. You know very well—"

"I know that I swore to you that your daughter would be married to a prince," Liall finished for him, putting out some volume of his own. If Ressanda wanted to deal with his king like a merchant bawling over a cargo of fish, he could do the same. "We both know that prince was to be Cestimir. Fate has a strange way with men's lives. And women's." He paused. "Speaking of japes, Jarad Hallin was a poor one. I hope he enjoys shoveling shit, for that's where he'll be until winter. Pity, but I doubt you'll miss him."

Ressanda dug in and refused to be distracted from his target. "Even so, I have come for my daughter's wedding."

"A king is not a bull and you are not a drover, ser, to be chivvying me to the breeding barn!" Liall slammed his wine cup on the table and green wine splashed over the scuffed wood. "You came because you were bloody well sent for, and you knew what would happen if you refused. I have more important matters to consider than your haste to marry off a daughter."

Ressanda's cheeks reddened as if slapped. "My daughter could assure your dynasty, the continuance of the house of Camira-Druz. Is that so little?"

Liall forced himself to count to three before replying. Ressanda had a point. There were many women at court who would be happy to take on the job of mother to a crèche of royal heirs, but beyond his cousin Winotheri and her daughter Ressilka, there were few Camira-Druz left. Ressanda spoke the truth.

"I meant no disrespect to the lady," Liall said carefully. "In my temper, I misspoke. The lady's marriage is indeed a great matter. One that I will address in time."

"How much time?" the baron pressed.

"As much as I say," Liall snapped. "I will marry when I please, and none of your growling will make the day come any sooner."

"What stands in your way, my king?"

Liall did not care for this direction. "Perhaps I just do not prefer women in my bed."

It wasn't far from the truth. Liall had never objected to a pretty woman between the sheets, but the rough-handed Jarek was more suited to him sexually than Shikhoza ever was, though Shikhoza had once been known as the most beautiful woman in Rshan. Ressilka was clever enough, but Tesk had informed him she was reserved and distant, prone to silences, and full of the same chilly dignity that his mother had possessed. She would have been perfect for Cestimir. Liall doubted she could hold his interest for long. Virginity is piquant in the young, and he had to admit he wasn't altogether indifferent to the thought of Ressilka naked, but he couldn't see himself sharing a life with her, or loving her. She would be looking for a gallant king to court her, to treat her honorably and pledge himself to her, and the most he could offer was a turn under the covers to get her with child before he returned to Scarlet's arms.

Not without breaking Scarlet's heart.

"I believe there is another impediment," Ressanda said.

"My t'aishka is not an impediment," Liall said quietly.

"And whoever claims so risks my wrath. You forget yourself, ser: A t'aishka is a chosen love, life to life, closer than blood. I have known him before."

"Superstition," Ressanda scoffed. "Fairytales and bedtime stories! We have no proof of these other lives, just as there is no proof of gods or demons or magic."

"And yet many have witnessed ser Keriss's magic. Account for that, my lord, if you can. Or, if you truly believe it is trickery, I will call for ser Keriss and he can demonstrate his powers for you. That matter is closed."

"I have learned that Hilurin are short-lived—"

Liall's look was so coldly furious that Ressanda closed his mouth at once.

"If you finish that sentence, I will have you turned out of the city like a common beggar," Liall warned, his mind a blaze of anger. "And if you value your neck, you will not seek to make his life any shorter than it already is." *And you should thank the Shining Ones that you did not call him a lenilyn.*

"You suggest that I would stoop to assassination?" Ressanda sputtered, and Liall could see that the baron was setting up to work himself into one of his famous rages.

"If you cannot calm yourself, my lord, then you should go back to Tebet and stay there. When the Ava Thule are howling at your gates, do not call to me for aid. My protection does not extend to traitors."

"Traitors!" Ressanda blew his breath out and shook himself all over like a wet dog. "I do not care for the way you treat your barons, my lord."

My lord. Far short of "my king". When Liall had known

Ressanda in his youth, the baron never failed to name him prince.

"And I do not care to be forced to call one of my sworn barons twice to my side. Your displeasure is noted. Be sure you make note of mine." Liall sipped his wine while Ressanda stewed. "Are you done showing me your fangs?"

Liall could see Ressanda biting his cheek on his reply. "Done, my king."

That's better. Good dog. Liall knew he must never let Ressanda forget who held the power. Ressanda was not a pure Rshani, and Morturii were infamous power-mongers. *He's had the whip, time to try the carrot.*

"In time, when the fighting is done and the realm settled, there may be a place for your daughter at my court," Liall said. "Haste will not make the Lady Ressilka any dearer to me. Besides, the Ava Thule may have my head on a pole by this time next year. Be sure they'd seek my queen's neck soon after. You may be hastening your daughter to a marriage that ends with her a hunted widow, ser. Or a corpse. Let me settle my kingdom before I settle a crown on a queen."

Ressanda took this for capitulation. Victory suffused his features before he bowed shortly. "As my king wishes."

Liall motioned for him to sit and called for more wine. "I trust your journey was not too tiresome?" he asked politely. *It costs nothing to be polite*, he thought. *Please is not a promise.*

Ressanda settled his bulk into the keg-chair. "It is a swift journey by sea," he said warily. "The captain said the currents favored us, and that he had never made the port of Sul in such a short time. He declared it a good omen." He shrugged.

"Perhaps it is."

Liall remembered that he had liked Ressanda for most of his life. The baron had made many wise choices for his people, and had always been loyal to the queen. He was brusque and demanding and overly proud of his splash of royal blood, but he was not a coward or a liar.

Ressilka had been promised—albeit never formally—to a prince of Rshan, and had dwelled at the royal court for more than three years. It was rumored that she was a bitter rival of Shikhoza's, as well as many other of the court ladies who envied Ressilka her royal name and her beauty. One did not thrive in such an environment unless one was very shrewd. Cestimir had appreciated Ressilka, and Cestimir had been no fool.

No, no fool; just sad and doomed, Liall thought glumly. *Doomed and running to his fate with open arms.*

He wondered if Ressilka had the same fatalistic tendencies as his late half-brother. He hoped not.

"Omen or no, it is good that we meet on friendly terms," Liall said courteously. "My brother spoke of Lady Ressilka often with affection. I do believe Cestimir loved her." He watched Ressanda carefully.

The baron sighed, his belly heaving like an ocean. "As she loved him, my king. He was a noble prince, and very intelligent. I admired him greatly. He always knew the right thing to do."

Ouch. Liall smirked. "He was noble and gentle," he allowed. "I am not my brother, baron. No more than you are your great grandmother. Tell me: does Ressilka *want* to marry me?"

Ressanda gave him a sharp look. "It is her duty, sire. I wish for her to wed, so she shall wed, if it please the king."

"So she has no affection for me?" Liall pressed.

Ressanda pulled at his short beard. "She has a great affection for the king. I have told her that you would be a dutiful and excellent husband, and that you will make her happy."

"I've never made any woman happy," Liall said flatly. "I've taken women as lovers, but it never lasted. Now my heart is claimed by another, and I have a bond with him that cannot be broken in this life. Even if there were a marriage, even if there were children, I could not love her. I'm already in love."

"If that is so, then that is how it must be, alas for her." Ressanda toyed with the stem of his wine cup. Liall thought he might have looked ashamed. "She will obey you, and she will have her court and her ladies to keep her company, and children to return her love. Is that not enough?"

"That's something you'll have to take up with her."

Ressanda shrugged. "Happy or not, she must carry on my line with a man worthy of her. She is a lady of the blood, sire, and it is her fate."

Fate.

Liall pushed back his chair. As one, the hall stood. "My lord, the meeting is at an end," he said, eyes sweeping the assembled. "I give you the freedom of Sul, baron. My people are at your disposal for the length of your stay, but I and my t'aishka depart the morning after next. The soldiers I have commanded from you should assemble at Starhold. They must be present and ready to depart north when I give the command, or I shall know I have lost an ally." *And then the Shining Ones help you. You spoke true, Ressanda. I am a Camira-Druz. We do not forget our enemies.*

Ressanda bowed. "My king is generous."

Liall gave him a nod of dismissal and turned to go.

"But I think…"

Irritated, Liall turned back to him. "Yes?" he asked, an edge in his voice.

"But I think," Ressanda began again, "that perhaps you do young ser Keriss an injustice. Even in Tebet, we have heard of his courage and wit. He has become accustomed to far stranger things than a mere wife. Look how he thrives here, among folk so alien to him."

Liall grunted. He wouldn't have said Scarlet was thriving, but neither would he tip Ressanda and his nobles off to that fact. He decided to let the baron have his say. "It is so. Ser Keriss is remarkable."

"Your t'aishka may not like Ressilka at first, but she is prepared to be a friend to him, my lord. To be his family as you are his family, to show respect and affection, and hopefully one day have that affection returned. I can swear to you that she has no thoughts of maneuvering him from your household."

"Good. She would fail, and would maneuver herself out of a crown as well. He's the other half of my heart, and anyone who hopes to be included in my life had better get used to that."

"There is one other matter, sire," Ressanda said tactfully.

Gods, would this man never learn when he was dismissed? "Yes? Out with it."

"There is a lady in my company who has requested a word with you. Will you grant it?

Braying barons, loving brides, and now tittering ladies-in-waiting. What an awful day. Liall shrugged. "Why not? She can find me lodged in Bleakwatch tower, waiting to see Tebet's colors on the backs of the men you owe me. Good day, my lord."

Liall turned and left abruptly. He had not given his promise to marry, but he'd not rejected Ressilka outright, either. He had left the matter open deliberately, left Tebet dangling in hope.

He strode to the stairs and took them two at a time, Alexyin following. He climbed the high stone steps until they curved sharply and opened up into a wide, low room with stone buttresses supporting the ceiling. An iron-banded door opened to the battlements, and Liall made for it. He felt the need for cleaner air.

Cannon lined the ramparts, well-oiled and gleaming black in the light. A brisk rush of salt air hit Liall's face like a cold slap. The sun was low in the sky and gave no warmth, but after months of darkness, it was as good as a blazing day on the Nerit.

"Was that wise, my king?" Alexyin's face was pinched.

Liall shrugged. "Wise or no, he will not press me further this year at least, and we can count on his soldiers."

"And next year?"

"Next year can hang or fuck itself blind." Liall gritted his teeth. "Is not one nobleman pushing me between a woman's legs enough? I do not need you to remind me of my duty, ser. I drank in duty at my lady mother's breast. In politics, one never says *no* outright. Much better to say *perhaps*, or *in the future*, or *another day*. *'No'* gives them nowhere to turn, and no room for me to do some maneuvering of my own. I am the king of Rshan, not your student to scold. Those days are past."

Alexyin bowed to him stiffly. "My lord king."

"Oh, stop it." Liall leaned his elbows on a parapet and looked down. Far below them, Ressanda's retinue were assembling to depart Arrowgate, the baron striding before his guards like a bear on the trail of meat.

"If I don't marry Ressilka," Liall said, "I'll have to be very careful in choosing a man for her. If I do marry her, I will have to watch her ambitious father very closely." He saw that Alexyin relaxed at his words.

Because I said 'if'. People hear only what they want to hear. Scarlet could have heard the lie in my words. He would have challenged me on it, and named me liar to my face if I hurt him. Well, I will not hurt him again, and I will not lose him. No matter what it costs me, he will not die.

Liall heard soft footsteps behind him, the whisper of silken skirts over stone. The lady-in-waiting. He turned, a courtesy already on his lips for her greeting, and stopped dead-still.

"You may go, Alexyin," he commanded.

Alexyin was staring, but he bowed to Liall and to the

lady before he hurriedly took his leave. Liall did not blame him.

She was wearing a gown in summer yellow and ivory with a starred veil over her breasts. Her hair was unbound and unadorned, falling nearly to her knees in a silken mass of pale gold. She was thinner. Her eyes, though, had not changed in the least. They were still the coldest eyes in Rshan.

Liall waited for her curtsy. She managed to make it look obedient.

"Lady Shikhoza. You travel with Baron Ressanda as his companion now?"

"My lord husband would not approve of that, would he?" Shikhoza smiled.

"What Eleferi would approve of is irrelevant, since you hold the purse-strings to his barony. Tell me, my lady, is that jingling sound his balls? How lonely they must be in your wallet, with only silver to clasp them and keep them warm."

She had the grace to smile artfully and defer with another curtsy, and Liall saw that she was still a great beauty, though not as great as she had been. As a girl, Shikhoza had been able to reduce grown men to tears. She was younger than him by a few years, but now she looked older.

It must truly be as bad as they say in Uzna Minor. She looks pinched and frightened. What could frighten Shikhoza?

"I'm sorry to have displeased you, my king. Would—"

He cut through the rest of it. "Just tell me why you're here. You've not come out of love for your king, certainly. What are you after?"

Shikhoza sighed. "I am here, my lord, because Baron Ressanda asked me to accompany his daughter to court, to act as her chaperone and advise her as a matron. A young girl hoping to wed has need of such advice."

"Good gods," he exclaimed. "A matron now, is it? Deva save the poor child if she takes advice from you. I don't want you here. Tell your craven husband that when you return to him. He'll weep with joy to have you back at his side."

"Eleferi agreed that it was important I go."

"To pressure me to make a girl once promised to my brother a queen of Rshan?"

Shikhoza's smile turned cutting. "Lady Ressilka is three years older than your consort. If she is a child, what does that make him?"

He had walked right into that one. Why did he allow her so much ammunition? Was it guilt, still, after all these years?

"Careful, my lady. Scarlet is a grown man, as you well know."

"Yes, but such a young one. So trusting, so naive. And so very fragile. Did you always lust for such delicate bedmates, or is that a taste you acquired among the *lenilyn?*"

Her tone chilled him. *One quick shove,* he thought. She'd be over the wall and he'd be free of her venom. "Your games didn't work on me when I was fifteen. I assure you that I've not grown softer in my prime. Have you grown nostalgic, I wonder? Did you come all this way just to bore me with your jealousy?"

She still had a musical laugh. "You think I'm jealous of an illiterate peasant boy?"

"You're jealous of a man who has everything you ever wanted and could not attain. And yes, you hate him all the more because of what he is. Because of *who* he is. You wanted a crown. He will have it instead."

Shikhoza stopped laughing. "You'd make a mockery of the bonds of marriage?"

"Lady, you pledged your hand to me but fucked my brother. You're the queen of mockery." Liall's mouth curled. "No, I will not wed Scarlet. No mere marriage can equal the bond of t'aishka. Still, I have no intention of infuriating my people and dishonoring my lineage by mixing the blood of my ancestors with that of *Kalaslyn.*"

Her lips parted in shock. "You speak of Lady Ressilka? She is a Camira-Druz."

"In name only. She has as much Morturii blood as Rshani. There are other ladies from purer stock. Not so royal, true, but not so red, either. My children should *look* Rshani at least." Liall wondered if Shikhoza would scramble to tell Ressanda that juicy tidbit first, or if she'd save it up for a rainy day. She wouldn't think he was lying. Shikhoza was snob enough for ten kings and never hesitated to believe the same of others.

She thinks me unchanged, Liall realized. She still saw him through the lens of those years when he was young and foolish, when it was just the three of them: Shikhoza and Nadei and himself, the second-born. He was prideful then, so very proud.

Shikhoza pressed a hand to her throat and was silent for several moments. "Perhaps…" she whispered with a backward glance at the door, "perhaps it is not wise to look for fruit so far from the tree." She lifted her chin and her eyes met his. "It is a great pity we never had a child, you and I."

"But we didn't," he retorted. Shikhoza's eyes were so pale they were almost colorless. *Like chips of diamond,* he thought. Those were Scarlet's words.

Shikhoza's lips turned up like the petals of a flower. "Did we not?"

Liall forced himself not to take the bait, not to react, but his heart began to thump harder. "We did not. I would have known. The queen would have known."

Shikhoza put her gloved hand on the stone battlement and glided a little nearer to him. "Your lady mother had just lost both of her sons, one to death and one to exile. It was a marvel she did not lose her mind, much less fail to notice the condition and whereabouts of a woman she despised."

"The queen would have known," Liall repeated. "And you are on the verge of committing a crime."

"Of telling the king a truth he doesn't want to hear?"

"There is *no* child," Liall said through his teeth.

As fast as she had pressed, Shikhoza seemed to relent. She looked down and rearranged her starred veil. "If the king says there is not, then there is not. Nadei would have been overjoyed at the possibility."

"Silence!" Liall shouted. He clenched his fists, truly afraid of what he might do if she kept talking. It was one thing to play these games with him, but the phantom heir she conjured might as well have been a bolt aimed at Nadei.

She lied. The bitch lied. When did she ever tell me the truth?

He and Shikhoza had been promised to each other as children, but from the very beginning she had toyed with him like a cat with a mouse between her claws. It was a short game, for he would not play it. Luckily, most of his waking hours were consumed with training and study, and when he became a man her schemes lost their sting, becoming familiar and tiresome to him. He turned from her and sought more pleasurable company, allowing his name to become known in the brothels of Sul. It was that year that she turned her fangs on Nadei, seducing him, baiting him, wounding his pride, teasing him, setting brother against brother at every turn.

"When I won at swords," he choked out, "you sneered and pretended to pity him. When he won a race, you told him I could have done better. You broke his heart a hundred times. You tortured him, and for what? I loved him and he never knew it. He would never believe it, all because of you. He's gone and you have gained *nothing!*" A wolf-like growl surged up in his throat. His arm shot out and he wrapped his fingers around her throat. It was a supreme effort not to squeeze. He seized her by the back of her hair and pulled her so close he could see the silver flecks in her eyes, wide with sudden terror.

Liall bared his teeth. "Every breath from your mouth is poison." Before true berserker rage could take over his mind, he shoved her so hard that her hip crashed against a parapet and she fell to her knees.

"Nazir," she quavered, covering her throat with her hands. "My king. I've never told you. It was not what you believe with… with Nadei. I never wanted—"

"Shut up." He stood over her, shaking. "On pain of

death, never come into my presence again," he commanded. "If I ever set eyes on you after today, I will kill you."

In the hall, he pushed past Alexyin. "I've had enough of liars today. Seek me at the tower if I'm needed."

Alexyin glanced at the iron-banded door, his brow creased with worry. "Sire, the lady—"

"I said enough!"

At the tower, Liall found Scarlet seated on the floor with a white bearskin around his shoulders, staring into the embers of the hearth. Liall strode to him and seized him by his arms, hauling him up.

"Liall?"

Liall's mouth found Scarlet's and his tongue thrust inside. He heard a door close in the hall. Margun had been ordered to stay nearby. Scarlet heard it, too.

Scarlet pulled away and pushed small hands against Liall's chest. "They can hear… we shouldn't…"

"I don't give a damn what the guards hear," Liall answered. "Let them hear. Let the whole bloody tower hear."

He kissed Scarlet again hungrily, and his hands began pulling at Scarlet's clothes, jerking at the laces in front of his breeches.

"Liall," Scarlet protested, weaker than before, breathless, his eyes narrowed as he smiled. With a moan, he gave in, wrapping his arms around Liall and melting against him. Liall slid his hand through Scarlet's silken hair and kissed him, holding him tight.

The bearskin was deep and soft. Against Scarlet's white skin it was snow against snow. Liall tore away what clothing he could not negotiate and covered Scarlet's slender body with his own. Now it was snow against amber.

The first time was desperate and hurried. He was rough, he knew, with his breeches around his ankles and his boot-toes scraping the floor, Scarlet's back against his belly. He thrust into Scarlet's body with his mouth close to Scarlet's ear, gasping and whispering words of love. His hands curled around Scarlet's shoulders and he was careful, ever so careful, not to bruise him.

I'll never cause him pain, he swore silently. *I will kill anyone who does.*

Scarlet's cries were loud and ecstatic, and the sound of them made Liall's skin tingle and his body taut with lust, that he could force such beautiful sounds from his lover.

"Yes?" he murmured into Scarlet's ear.

"Yes." Scarlet moaned and pushed back against him. "More."

Liall's hand slid to cup Scarlet's chin, to slip his fingers inside that lovely mouth. "My t'aishka."

Later, the second time, Scarlet sat astride his hips as he liked to do and rode him, hands on Liall's shoulders, Liall looking up in rapture. It was Scarlet's way of taking *him,* of finding a measure of control in their unequal statures, and Liall loved it.

"That's it," Liall moaned, his hands on Scarlet's thighs as he watched through narrowed eyes heavy with lust. "That's it, my love, that's it. I'm yours, take me, take all of me, take all of me and forever…"

To be continued in "Scarlet and the White Wolf, Book 5: The Temple Road"

.

ABOUT THE AUTHOR

Kirby Crow is an American writer born and raised in the Deep South. She is a winner of the EPIC Award and the Rainbow Award, and is the author of the bestselling *Scarlet and the White Wolf* series of fantasy novels. Kirby and her husband and their son share an old, lopsided house in the Blue Ridge with a cat. Always a cat.

More Books by Kirby Crow

Prisoner of the Raven
Scarlet and the White Wolf, Book 1: The Pedlar and the Bandit King
Scarlet and the White Wolf, Book 2: Mariner's Luck
Scarlet and the White Wolf, Book 3: The Land of Night
Scarlet and the White Wolf, Book 4: The King of Forever
Angels of the Deep
Circuit Theory
Hammer and Bone
Poison Apples Turks Cay
Malachite, Book 1 of the Paladin Cycle
Meridian (Mirror Series #1)
Windward (Mirror Series #2)

Coming Soon

Scarlet and the White Wolf, Book 5: The Temple Road
Crossbones, Book 2 of the Paladin Cycle

A romantic retelling of a classic fairytale...

Scarlet of Lysia is an honest pedlar, a young merchant traveling the wild, undefended roads to support his aging parents. Liall, called the Wolf of Omara, is the handsome, world-weary chieftain of a tribe of bandits blocking a mountain road that Scarlet needs to cross. When Liall jokingly demands a carnal toll for the privilege, Scarlet refuses and an inventive battle of wills ensues, with disastrous results.

Scarlet is convinced that Liall is a worthless, immoral rogue, but when the hostile countryside explodes into violence and Liall unexpectedly fights to save the lives of Scarlet's family, Scarlet is forced to admit that the Wolf is not the worst ally he could have, but what price will proud Scarlet ultimately have to pay for Liall's friendship?

An adventurous trek through a harsh fantasy world filled with magic, myth, earthy heroes, relentless villains, and an unconventional relationship that shines a new light on a beloved old fable.

Learn more at
http://KirbyCrow.com

Made in the USA
Coppell, TX
10 March 2020

16701454R00141